Horse Whispers
in the Air

Dandi Daley Mackall

CPH.
SAINT LOUIS

Horsefeathers

Horsefeathers!
Horse Cents
Horse Whispers in the Air
A Horse of a Different Color
Horse Angels
Home Is Where Your Horse Is
Horsefeathers' Mystery
All the King's Horses

Interest level: ages 12–16

All Scripture quotations are taken from the HOLY BIBLE, NEW INTERNATIONAL VERSION®. NIV®. Copyright © 1973, 1978, 1984 by International Bible Society. Used by permission of Zondervan Publishing House. All rights reserved.

Text copyright © 2000 Dandi Daley Mackall
Published by Concordia Publishing House
3558 S. Jefferson Avenue, St. Louis, MO 63118-3968
Manufactured in the United States of America

Library of Congress Cataloging-in-Publication Data

Mackall, Dandi Daley.
   Horse whispers in the air / Dandi Daley Mackall.
     p. cm.
  Summary: After she discovers what her grandfather had been collecting in jars which appeared to be enpty, Scoop understands that although he had Alzheimer's, he remembered the past.
   ISBN 0-570-07008-2
  [1. Grandfathers—Fiction. 2. Alzheimer's disease—Fiction.
  3. Christian life—Fiction.] I. Title.
  PZ7.M1905 Hr 2000
  [Fic]—dc 21
                           99-050884

2 3 4 5 6 7 8 9 10 11   10 09 08 07 06 05 04 03 02 01

This book is dedicated to my daughter,

Katy, who is always my first reader.

Thanks for catching all those mistakes!

1

"Scoop! Where's your grandaddy? I can't find him nowhere."

I blinked, hoping this was just a dream, that Dotty wasn't really standing over me in her pink, fuzzy robe and matching hair curlers, aiming her flashlight at my face. Rolling away from her, I drew my pillow over my head. "Horsefeathers, Grandad's not here," I mumbled through the pillow case.

I felt fingers on my shoulder, pushing and shaking me. "Scoop, he ain't in the house! You gotta help find him."

It was no use pretending to sleep, pretending my Alzheimer's-ridden grandfather hadn't taken off ... again. I groaned and tried to sit up, just as my aunt flipped on the bedroom light. I covered my eyes.

"Good," Dotty said, retreating from my tiny attic room and heading for the stairs. "I'll get B.C. to help search. You skedaddle to the barn. If Grandad ain't there, Orphan can help you look."

5

I heard her on the stairs, talking to God on the way down. "Lord, help us find that man before he catches hisself a death of cold."

I sat on the edge of the bed and tried to think. My feet touched the cold, wood floor, sending a shiver through me. Outside, branches scraped against the window. Great—cold *and* windy. I glanced at my alarm clock on the dresser. 3:10 A.M. Terrific. In three hours I'd be getting up anyway for my first day in high school. Off to a good start.

By the time I pulled jeans and a sweatshirt over my nightgown and pulled on boots over my bare feet, B.C. and Dotty were already outside. Over the howling of the wind, I could hear the duet of voices in the backyard—my brother's high, squeaky "Grandad!" and Dotty's off-key "Jared?" clashing in air.

I pulled on a jacket and stepped out the kitchen door. The night was black, but stars peeked through moving gray cloud swirls. "Dotty? Any luck?" I hollered.

B.C. trotted up, still in pajamas, his bushy brown hair sticking up like porcupine quills. "I'm cold," he said, his teeth chattering to prove it. "I'm not going to school tomorrow." My brother would be starting fourth grade, and he and school don't exactly get along.

"Make that *today*, B.C.," I said.

Dotty came lumbering up in her pink

bathrobe, which made her look even more plump than she is. Half of her curlers had fallen out, and her glasses looked fogged. "He ain't out back, Scoop. Hurry over to the barn. I'll get the Chevy and head the other way. B.C., where's your shoes? You get back inside before you catch the death of you! Lord Jesus, protect that man from the cold and hisself." Dotty said it all without taking a breath, switching her requests from me, to B.C., to Jesus, as natural as horseflies.

Wind blew my hair across my face—long, black strands that reminded me I'd forgotten to get my before-school haircut. I grabbed as many strands as I could and shoved them under my jacket collar. Then I stuck my hands in my pockets and walked fast, leaning into the wind all the way to the barn. I was too tired to be worried about Grandad. Besides, this was the fourth time in two weeks he'd wandered off. He always turned up.

Orphan whinnied as soon as I stepped into the lane at Horsefeathers Stable. She trotted to the fence and nodded her head at me, surprised by the late visit. A sliver of moonlight from the quarter moon fell on her beautiful black coat. She's a cross between a Saddlebred and a quarter horse. Most people think she looks like a Morgan.

"Nice to see you too, Orphan," I called. I met her at the fence and scratched her ears, pressing my cold, dry cheek to her fuzzy, warm one. It was barely September, but fall was trying to come early, making up for the hot summer we'd had. Orphan's hair had already gotten softer, a shade longer, and shaggier. I knew we'd get another warm spell and she'd lose the shagginess as quickly as she got it, until late fall, when her coat would become pure fur.

"Come help me find Grandad again," I said, soaking up her warmth as I hugged her neck. I broke away and ran to the barn. Only Ham nickered from inside, the only horse to take advantage of his stall and get out of the wind. Moby and Cheyenne wouldn't spend the night in the barn if you paid them in sugar cubes—not until dead winter anyway.

I flipped on the light. "Grandad!" I called, walking up and down the stallway, peering into every stall. My boots clumped and echoed in the barn. Outside an owl hooted and the wind still howled. I checked the office and the tack room. I even climbed to the hayloft, where our barn cat, Dogless, stayed curled up and snoozing. "Come out, come out wherever you are!" I shouted.

He wasn't there, which meant I'd have to hunt on Orphan. I took down a lead rope and met Orphan in her stall. She nickered and put her head down so I could clip the rope to her halter. I was so tired that I missed the first time I tried to swing up on her bare back. I couldn't quite pull myself up.

"Sorry, Orphan," I said. For some reason, that was the moment I remembered what else was happening tomorrow besides the first day of school. Horsefeathers Stable was getting a new horse, a paying customer. I'd have to rush back to the barn right after school to meet the owners. Getting the horse would be great, and we needed the extra boarding and training fee. It was the people I was worried about. I'm not very good talking to new people, and Carla Buckingham, who might have helped with that part, was still in Kentucky visiting her mother, who was getting a divorce from Carla's father. I should have been getting a good night's sleep. Instead, here I was in Orphan's stall in the middle of the night. *Horsefeathers*.

Orphan stood close to her feed trough, and I stepped onto her back, ducking my head fast as she walked out to the side pasture. I figured her horse sense was better than mine, so I let her find her own way in the dark. We covered pasture after pasture, with me yelling, "Grandad!"

It surprised me how well I could see in the dark pasture after we got away from the glow of the barn and my eyes adjusted to the starlight. Cheyenne, Jen's Paint, came charging toward us, then playfully veered away in the nick of time, just missing Orphan's side. Moby, Maggie's 23-

year-old mare, lifted her head to check us out, then lay down in the grass for a real sleep. The smell of grass mixed with clover blended dreamlike with the dew.

If it hadn't been for the anxious feeling seeping into me like the night chill, I would have loved the ride. Orphan has been my best friend for more than 11 years, since the year she was born, and the year my folks adopted me, when I was 3. She'd lived here at Horsefeathers her whole life, although it wasn't called Horsefeathers when Grandad had his horse farm. We've grown up together, and there's nothing I'd rather do than ride her—even in the middle of the night.

But I was starting to worry about Grandad. The other times he'd wandered out of the house, we'd found him in our yard or at the barn. But Orphan and I covered every pasture, and still no trace of him.

"We better go back," I said, willing Orphan toward the barn. She knew what I wanted and broke to a gentle canter, straight-lining us to the barn. When we got there, I hopped off and unhooked the lead rope. I felt bad for not brushing Orphan or picking her hooves, but I knew she'd understand.

"I'll see you before school, Girl," I whispered, kissing her white blaze.

I ran most of the way home, stopping to holler for Grandad, then praying as I ran again.

The sun was making the horizon lighter. I saw the old Chevy parked crooked in the lawn, half off the driveway. I couldn't decide if that was a good sign that Dotty was home, or a bad sign that she'd parked in a hurry. My heart pounded faster as I walked in the front door.

If there's such a thing as an opposite smell of the fresh night air, it was coming from our musty living room. Dotty meant to get the leak in the ceiling fixed. We left a metal bucket on the floor under the leak, and I could smell wet rust.

The door to Dotty's bedroom was closed except for a crack that leaked golden light. I heard shuffling inside and a drawer open and shut, Dotty getting ready for bed—or dressing for work, more likely.

I walked to the kitchen, where a faint light spilled out of the open refrigerator door. Somebody had set out all the jars of pickles—sweet pickles, dill pickles, sliced, whole—along with the mustard, peanut butter, and mayonnaise. The assortment of glass containers littered the counter on both sides of the sink.

"I got Grandad to bed. Sorry I sent you out for nothing," Dotty said.

I turned around and saw her wiggling into her orange Hy-Klas shirt, the one Mr. Ford makes all the checkout workers wear.

"Where was he?" I asked, knowing I should have asked *how* he was.

"You know, B.C. and I can't figure it. We was driving all around looking for him. When we got back, the door to the house was wide open and your grandad was in here, over at the sink, just setting all this stuff out of the ice box. He was real fussy. I liked to never get him back to bed."

Dotty walked to the sink. One pink curler peeked out of the back of her thinning brown hair. "I'll clean up here, Honey," she said, rolling up her sleeves. "You go get some shut-eye. I'll get you in half an hour. B.C., he done fell to sleep like a baby. And your grandaddy is in his room. He'll sleep this morning, I reckon. I'll see if Addy can look in on him. I'll come home on break. You get straight home after school—"

"I can't, Dotty!" I said, so loud, I said it again soft. "I can't. I told you. Right after school those cousins of Ray's are bringing their problem horse. I'm meeting them at Horse-feathers to get her settled in and see about helping the mare. I can't baby-sit Grandad! We can't keep doing this, Dotty. He's getting worse and you know it."

There. I'd said it. It's what I'd been thinking, what I was just plain too tired not to say.

Dotty didn't turn around. I had a feeling she was praying. "You go on to your horses. I just forgot, Scoop. I'll tend to Jared."

She turned to face me and wiped her hands on a dishtowel, leaning back on the enamel sink. "Grandad will get better. He'll come back to us, Scoop. You'll see."

"He hasn't even talked to us for weeks, Dotty, not to make any sense anyway. We shouldn't have to do everything by ourselves. Why can't you make Stephen's family help? The Daltons could afford to hire on help. They're the ones who should be watching out for Grandad."

Stephen Dalton's mom and my adoptive dad were Grandad's kids. My dad died in an explosion when I was 7. So did my mom. But Patricia Coop Dalton was still around. Why wasn't she taking care of her own dad? Even though the Daltons were filthy rich and had the fanciest stables in our part of the country, they never lifted a finger to help us with Grandad.

"You listen here to me, Scoop," Dotty said, softly but in her no-nonsense tone. "We'll take care of Jared on our own. All them Daltons need is to hear about something like what happened tonight, and they'll haul your grandaddy off to the old people's home in Kennsington. That's what they wanted all along. And that would kill Jared. He belongs here with us."

"But maybe—"

"No maybe about it. I got things I have to say to your grandad. He ain't going nowhere. If

I'm wrong, let God show me so Hisself. Until then, don't you go blabbing about this here at school. You hear?"

I sighed. Through the smudged kitchen window, the first rays of morning shone, pointing out that our windowpanes probably hadn't been washed since David slew Goliath.

I started to say something else to Dotty, but I heard somebody behind me. I turned in time to step out of the way. Grandad barreled into the kitchen and straight to the counter, where Dotty had started putting things away. Without a nod to either of us, Grandad picked up the jar of sweet pickles and studied it. Then before we could stop him, he opened it and dumped every last pickle, juice and all, directly on the floor.

Dotty rushed over with her towel and started cleaning it up. Grandad shuffled past me, the jar in one hand, the lid in the other. Going through the living room, he must have bumped B.C. or the couch as he shuffled through to his little bedroom.

B.C. screamed, "I hate school! I hate school! And I'm not going and you can't make me!"

As Dotty dumped the pickles in the garbage, I heard her mumbling to God, "Thanks again for keeping Jared safe. Give me that time and that talk with him. How about some Frosty Flakes?"

It took me a minute to figure out she was offering *me* the flakes. I gave up and plopped at the kitchen table as the sun kept climbing the sky on my first day of high school. I had a feeling it was going to be quite a year.

Maggie and Jen were waiting for me at West Salem High School. They both looked a hundred times more excited about ninth grade than I felt. Standing side by side, leaning on the brick building, they could have passed for high school kids.

Maggie and Jen are about as opposite as you can get. Maggie's brown skin matched everything she had on, from her close-fitting chocolate-brown dress to her medium brown shoes with straps that crossed at her ankles.

Jen, on the other hand, looked just about as white as a human can get—light blond hair like all nine Zucker children, fair skin, blue eyes, and today, white jeans and white cotton shirt.

My coloring is kind of between Maggie's and Jen's. I'm dark enough naturally that Ray sometimes calls me an Indian. And I'd spent so much time outside riding and working at Horsefeathers, my farmer's tan had grown deeper and darker. I wondered if I'd grown in any of the right ways over the summer, if I'd changed too.

Summer had been so busy I hadn't looked in the mirror much.

Maggie waved at me. "Scoop! Hurry!" She had no books. Jen, who carried a stack of at least six books even though we hadn't had a single class yet, lifted her chin to wave.

I joined them, and Maggie automatically smoothed my hair. "Scoop, isn't this the greatest! *We're* finally high school students! We rule! Just look at all these *people*!" Maggie bubbled on. "I'm on the entertainment committee. We're planning a mixer for this Friday night! It's going to be awesome! And I've already met four new cute guys! And have you seen Matthew lately? He must have been working out all summer."

She pulled something out of my braid, probably a piece of straw. I wondered if B.C. had given in and let Dotty comb his hair before school. I wondered if she'd gotten him to school. The good thing about B.C.'s manic depression is that it's like the weather around West Salem. If you don't like B.C.'s mood, just wait a spell. It can swing back as fast as a horse's tail.

I straightened my red pullover jersey and tugged at my blue jeans. "It took me longer than usual at Horsefeathers this morning," I said. "Moby and Cheyenne are fine, by the way. At least *they* got a good night's sleep."

"You don't look like you got any," Jen said,

squinting at me through her wire-rimmed glasses. "Your eyes are red."

Great. Just the look I was going for my first day of school. "Grandad," I said. I knew they'd figure the rest.

"Did you find him?" Maggie asked dramatically, always the actress.

"Did I hear the name of Grandad?" Stephen Dalton had snuck up behind us. He'd grown at least two inches over the summer. I didn't like having to look up to him. Stephen would be the best-dressed guy at school, if you like the preppy look. Shoes, shirt, belt, everything looked brand new. His pea green eyes narrowed at me, making him look like a snake. His red hair was combed to the side, and he smelled like hairspray. "So," he pressed, "what did the old coot do this time?"

"None of your business, Stephen," I said, as students bumped around us, jostling each other and laughing.

"Oh, it *is* my business!" Stephen declared. "Don't think we're not on to you and your aunt. We know why you took Grandad in. We're not stupid, Sarah!"

"That's open to debate," Maggie chimed in. Jen chuckled.

"What do you mean, Stephen? We took Grandad in because Dotty couldn't bear to see *your* family ship him off to a nursing home!"

"Sure you did," Stephen said, his thin upper

18

lip curving into a sneer that showed his retainer. "And it had *nothing* to do with the old man's will, I suppose?"

I felt like my blood was boiling and would explode any minute. "His will? Are you crazy? *You* were the ones who should have given him a home! Do you think it's fun taking care of him? If you're so worried about his money, why don't you come and get him?"

I hadn't meant to say it. I hadn't meant it, not really. But my mind felt like mush. All I wanted to do was go home and sleep. Stephen Dalton made me crazy.

The bell rang before Stephen could answer, and we were almost trampled by kids rushing in like a herd of sheep to the slaughter. Jen and Maggie and I were inside the door when I heard Stephen shout, "It won't work, Scoop! My dad's going for power of attorney!"

We didn't turn around. We acted like we hadn't heard Stephen. "What's he mean?" I whispered. "What's a *power of attorney?*"

Jen shifted her books, resting the stack on her knee before moving down the hall. "That's when the courts legally declare somebody unfit to handle his own money and things, so they turn it all over to his relative or his lawyer."

"That would be awful!" Maggie exclaimed. "Is your grandad really rich?"

"No way!" I said. "He was losing his horse

19

farm to the bank because of all his debts, remember? Stephen doesn't know what he's talking about. He probably heard about attorney power on TV."

We split down different halls. I didn't have the same homeroom as Jen and Maggie. Jen had all honors classes, so we didn't have anything together. Maggie and I had third hour gym, but nobody had my lunch period.

"Wait up!" Maggie cried down the hall. She trotted off into the side hall, stopping when she reached what looked like a football player. He turned to grin at Maggie. It was Matthew, and Maggie had been right about him working out all summer. I wondered if anybody would look at me and think I'd changed, grown up, or filled out. Probably not.

Then I remembered—the new horse was coming to Horsefeathers right after school. I needed help. Jen had already told me she had to go home after school and help the little Zuckers with homework. Maggie had promised to help, but if I didn't remind her, she wouldn't remember. "Maggie!" I hollered.

She turned around, one hand artfully placed on Matthew's arm so he couldn't get away. The other hand waved to me as she cocked her head to see me through the ocean of students pouring down the noisy halls.

"Horsefeathers after school!" I hollered.

"New horse! Be there!" If Carla had been there, I could have signed the message easily. She'd been teaching us how to do American Sign Language.

Maggie raised a fist in the air and moved it up and down—the sign for *yes*.

I nodded at some kids, said hi to others. I knew most of them, but it still felt lonely, maybe even worse because everybody else seemed so into school—seeing their friends again and making after-school plans.

Most of the time in classes, I just stared at my notebook or doodled things that ended up looking kind of like Orphan. And every morning class doled out homework as if that class were the only class I had to study for.

Even though I was starving by the time lunch came, I dreaded the cafeteria, teeming with groups of kids all glad to sit together. After I got my pizza, I looked around, then sat at an empty table in the corner, just about the only empty table left.

"Hey, Scoop." I looked up at Ray Cravens. He's tall, lanky, and as easygoing as a Tennessee Walking Horse. And he's about the only boy who doesn't make me tongue-tied. Ray's the one who got us the new business for Horsefeathers. He convinced his cousins to pull their horse out of Dalton Stables and try our stables.

"Hi, Ray," I said, hoping he couldn't see

how relieved I was to have somebody to talk to.

Ray sat down, his back to the table, his long legs stretched out. He wasn't carrying his tray. "You ready for my cousin's horse?" he asked, surveying the cafeteria as he talked.

"I will be," I said. "Will you come too, Ray? Please?"

He waved to somebody I couldn't see. "I don't know. Maybe. How's the Bottle Cap doing today?"

"B.C.? I don't know if Dotty got him to school or not."

Ray shook his head. I knew Ray liked my brother. But I had a suspicion this wasn't the real reason he'd stopped by the table.

"So, when are you expecting Carla back?" he asked.

That was it, the real reason. Something inside me wanted to cry. "I think she's staying with her mother for two more weeks. She's doing assignments on her own until then."

"Rats," Ray muttered. "You hear about the mixer Friday? I was hoping to go with her."

"The trip has been really good for both of them, Ray. I guess Carla's mother even asked her for forgiveness."

There was a lot that needed forgiving, but Carla said she told her mother that Christ's death paid for it all.

Ray frowned. "That's good. So there's no

chance she'll make it back in time?"

I shrugged. What was I? His dating service? I took a bite of the pizza. It tasted like cold tomato paste out of the can.

Ray left. The cafeteria felt hot and sticky. I wondered if the day had warmed outside like it had inside. A stench of green beans, tomato sauce, and silverware hovered over the room. Voices rose and sounded louder, as if the school were on fire but nobody cared enough to leave. Laughter came in explosions. At the nearest table, some ninth-grade girls giggled. It felt like they were laughing at me, although I knew they weren't. Nobody even noticed I was there. The cafeteria was as crowded as an ant hill ... except for my empty table.

I stared at the pizza I couldn't eat and prayed that God would forgive me for forgetting to bless the food before I tried to eat it. My stomach made it perfectly clear that if I sent it one more bite of anything, it would send everything right back up.

"*There* you are! I thought you had this period." It was Maggie in her Southern accent.

"Maggie? I thought you had first lunch period." I was so glad to see her I could have jumped up on the table and given her a big hug. I restrained myself.

She set down her tray of salad and applesauce. "That was before I dropped Spanish class.

That teacher was no fun at all." Maggie slid in across from me, then raised up and waved at somebody behind me. "Here! Come sit by me!"

A tall, lean, handsome African American guy set his tray next to Maggie and sat down. "Thanks," he said. "Toughest part of a new school is the cafeteria." He had an amazing smile, and it was aimed right at Maggie.

"Frank and I have several classes together," Maggie said. "But we haven't been formally introduced." Maggie shook his hand. "I'm Maggie 37 Brown. Thirty-seven was my mother's lucky number, and I was born on March 7. That's 3-7. And that's my middle name. We're glad to have you at West Salem High School, Frank. This is Scoop—actually Sarah Coop, but nobody in their right mind calls her Sarah."

"Pleased to meet both of you," Frank said, not taking his eyes off Maggie.

The table, which had been empty except for me, now filled up as if the music had suddenly stopped in a game of musical chairs. Ninth-grade boys vied for a seat near Maggie 37.

"Scoop is a teenaged horse whisperer. I was just about to fill her in on our mixer." Maggie measured salad dressing in her teaspoon and dripped it on her lettuce.

"Mixer?" Frank asked.

I had a feeling that Maggie was more interested in filling Frank in on the mixer than she was on filling me in. "This Friday night we're having a ninth-grade mixer. Frank, here in West Salem parties are scarcer than hen's teeth. So you just can't afford to miss one."

"Are you from the South, Maggie? You've got a Southern drawl, don't you?" Frank asked.

"Not really," she said, keeping the accent up. "I'm just practicing accents. I'm going to be an actress."

Frank was handsome enough to be an actor. And he didn't seem stuck on himself either. Good for Maggie—except I already saw her life filling up and pulling her away from Horsefeathers.

That's the thought that stuck in my head through the rest of my classes. Things were changing, friends were changing, and I was the only one holding on. By the end of school, all I wanted to do was hug my horse, smell her, and know that at least one thing in my life was still the same.

3

Horsefeathers, Maggie 37!" I muttered to myself. "Where are you?"

There was no one in the barn to hear me except Orphan and Dogless Cat. The new horse was scheduled to arrive around 4:00, which was only five minutes away. I should have known better than to trust Maggie to get to Horsefeathers on her own. Right after school, I'd tried to pull her away from the throngs of kids crowding around her like ants on a sugar lump. Finally, she'd convinced me to go on ahead without her. And now I'd be stuck greeting the new people by myself. Even Maggie's horse, Moby, didn't come in from the back pasture.

Inside the barn, Orphan kept getting in my way as I shoveled the last bit of muck from her stall. Dogless Cat rubbed at my ankles, tripping me, as if conspiring with everybody else to make my life impossible.

I dashed outside hoping for any sign of Maggie. A crow cawed from a ginkgo tree. Two rabbits scurried under a low bush. But Maggie

37 wasn't there. When I turned back to the barn, I tried to see Horsefeathers like the new people might see it. *The old gray barn ain't what she used to be*, I thought.

It hadn't been all that long since my grandfather ran the place like a real business. Grandad had kept more than 30 horses on the grounds, breeding and training quarter horses mostly. His whole farm had been in tip-top shape. Now the barn leaned just a bit toward the willow tree that overhung the roof. It looked like what it was—a barn, with real barn wood, rough and gray, paint flaking. Slats had been hammered around one window to square it up. I doubted the new clients would be impressed.

On the other hand, if I were a horse, even a new horse, I'd feel relieved at the sight of Horsefeathers Stable, a home where stall doors hung open, allowing horses to go in and out as they pleased. The barn smelled warm and earthy, and the pastures clean as fresh grass. I sent up a quick prayer of thanks to God for Horsefeathers.

I glanced up at our brand-new sign. Carla had painted it for us before she left to visit her mother. The board was white with big, black letters that read: HORSEFEATHERS—HOME OF THE BACKYARD HORSES. Carla wanted to write something about where a horse can be a horse, but she ran out of room.

B.C. made us a sign too—out of bottle caps. You couldn't really make out more than a couple of letters here and there, but I'd hung it up in the office anyway.

"Scoop!"

I wheeled around to see Jen Zucker biking up the path. I'd never been more glad to see her. "Jen? You came!" I trotted down the lane to meet her. "I can't believe you're here." I walked her to the barn, where she leaned her bike against the side wall.

"Travis got home without homework and actually volunteered to help Tommy with his spelling assignment and to stay home until Mom got back from town." Jen took a deep breath. She must have pedaled fast. "Where's Maggie?"

"That's what I'd like to know," I said. "I was afraid I'd be the only one here when the new horse showed up. Tell Travis thanks for covering for you, Jen." Travis is Jen's older brother. He has a driver's license and everything. If Travis were a horse, he'd be a stallion, probably a Palomino with strong bloodlines.

Jen sauntered over to the fence and called her horse, Cheyenne, over. The Paint lifted her head from the clover she was munching and stared at Jen, trying to decide between her owner and her clover. "Travis knew Ray was bringing us a new client," Jen said.

Client. It had a strange sound to it. So far, the only clients I'd had at Horsefeathers were my best friends—Jen, Maggie, and Carla ... and myself. This horse would be the first official boarder. And the owners were actual clients who wanted me to help "fix" their horse.

"Fill me in on our client again before they get here," Jen said, pulling up a handful of grass to lure Cheyenne over.

I whistled for Cheyenne, and she finally gave in and sauntered over to us, taking her time about it. I tried to remember everything Ray had told me and what Mr. Cravens had said over the phone. "She's a dapple gray mare, 15 years old, with—"

"Scoop," Jen said, straightening my shirt and brushing something off my shoulder. Her own shiny, blond hair was pulled back in a ponytail that reminded me of Barbie's hair. "Not the horse. Tell me about the owners."

"Ah," I said, searching my brain for that info. "Ray said his uncle bought the mare for their daughter Caroline to show. I think she's the same age as B.C.—9 or 10. Anyway, the Cravens have been keeping their horse at Dalton Stables for two months, ever since they bought her at auction."

"Poor horse," Jen said. She scratched Cheyenne behind the ears, and the grateful Paint closed her eyes and stretched her big, beautiful head at Jen. "So why did they decide to try Horsefeathers?"

"I'm not sure," I admitted, my stomach starting to feel like horses trotting inside. "Ray never said why they were switching from Dalton Stables exactly—just that the mare needed to be turned into a good riding horse. I was so happy to get another boarder—especially one from Dalton—I guess I didn't ask many questions."

"Didn't want to look a gift horse in the mouth?" Jen suggested. "Just as well. We need this money, Scoop. I'll bet Stephen and his dad are furious to see that horse go."

Orphan trotted along the fence, her ears pricked and tail held high.

"Someone's coming," I said. "I hope it's Maggie."

Far down the road a tan station wagon pulling a matching trailer came into view.

"It's the clients," Jen whispered.

I couldn't speak, couldn't think. My mouth went dry as I watched them pull up the lane and stop a few feet from Jen and me.

A lanky man got out of the passenger's seat, and a lean, redheaded women stepped out from behind the wheel. Ray and his cousins climbed out of the backseat.

"Four walking horses and a Shetland," I

whispered to Jen. That's what they would have been if they'd been horses. "You take the people, and I'll get the horse."

"No way!" Jen whispered back, shoving me forward. "Where is Maggie when we need her?"

I forced myself to smile. "Hello. Welcome to Horsefeathers." My voice sounded thin and frightened.

Mr. Cravens frowned at me, as if he couldn't figure out what I was doing there. I started to hold out my hand to shake his, then let it drop to my side. I opened my mouth, but nothing came out.

Ray came to my rescue. "Scoop, this is my Uncle Bob and Aunt Donna." We nodded at each other. "This little squirt is Caroline." He put his hand on top of her head.

"I'm not a squirt, Ray," she said. She was definitely bigger than B.C. and looked older than fourth grade. Her brown hair was smooth, in what Maggie would have deemed a "good cut"—if she'd been there. Her eyes looked like small triangles, but it may have been because she was squinting up toward the sun.

"Uncle Bob," Ray said, "this is Jen Zucker. And this is Sarah Coop, Scoop, the teenaged horse whisperer."

"This is Sarah Coop?" Ray's uncle didn't sound pleased.

Ray's aunt didn't look too happy about me either. "It's just ... we thought you'd be older," she said. She glanced uneasily at her husband. "Ray's father said you were young. I just didn't think you'd be *this* young. I guess we should have asked."

I swallowed and tried to look older. We really needed this horse to make next month's payment on the barn.

Ray's cousin walked around the front of the car, and I got my first good look at him. He was no Walking Horse after all. He could have been a Lusitano, the strong, agile mount preferred by Portuguese bullfighters. He had Ray's grin that came from big, brown eyes, rather than from his mouth. But his build was stockier than Ray's— more filled out, Dotty would say.

"I'm Jake," he said. "And I, for one, am glad you're not older. Why didn't you tell me Scoop was so pretty, Ray? Afraid I'd cut into your action?"

I felt Jen's elbow in my rib and realized Jake was holding out his hand for me to shake. I shook his hand, then realized my palms were sweaty. I wiped them on my jeans, then wondered if it looked like I was wiping off Jake's handshake.

"You won't find anybody better for helping your horse with whatever trouble you're having," Jen said, clearing her throat twice in order to get the words out. "Give Scoop a chance, Mr. and Mrs. Cravens, and you'll see for yourself."

Caroline still stood close to Ray, but she kept her gaze fixed on me. I walked over to her, hearing the scuff of my boots in the dirt. She wasn't much shorter than me, but I leaned down so we were eye to eye. "Caroline," I said, "I know it's hard to trust anybody with something as valuable as a horse. But I can promise you one thing—I'll do everything I can to understand your horse and to help her be the best friend you ever had."

Caroline bit her bottom lip and narrowed her eyes to slits. I didn't think she was going to answer. Then she said, "Can you really do that?"

I swallowed hard and said the world's fastest prayer that God would help me do just that. "I think I can," I said. "But I'm going to need your help. Is that okay?" My heart was pounding so loud I was afraid they'd all hear it.

Caroline glanced up at Ray, then back at me. Tears swam in the corners of her triangle eyes. "Okay," she said. "But you have to help my horse." She peeked back at her dad. "Because my dad says if you can't fix her, we have to sell her."

4

"Caroline, honey," said her dad, walking up and putting an arm around her. "We've been all over this." I could tell he loved her just by the way his forehead wrinkled when he talked to her. I wondered what that would be like, to wrinkle a father's brow like that. I pushed the thought out of my head.

"We got the mare for you because you wanted to show in 4-H shows," Mr. Cravens said. "Remember? If we can't get this mare to perform, then we'll get you another mare who can. There's no sense wasting money on a horse you can't show."

Caroline shrugged at her dad, then turned back to me. "I can't get her to do anything," she said. "All she'll do is walk or stop. She's so lazy I can't get her to canter at all."

"That's why we brought her to Scoop, isn't it, Squirt?" Jake said. "She'll come around."

I peeked into the trailer at the mare, who wore a burgundy, silk utility blanket and an undercover that covered her neck and face like

34

nylon panty hose. Big black eyes and droopy ears poked out of the face covering. She stood about 14.2 hands and was a rich dapple gray. "What's her name?" I asked.

"Little Sugar General," Caroline said. "Sugar for short."

I moved to the back of the trailer and got a better look at the mare. Even though Sugar was cooped up in strange surroundings, hearing voices and noises she couldn't investigate, she stood perfectly still, not even looking around at me.

"Bet she rode real quiet, didn't she?" I asked.

"She does everything real quiet," Caroline said, in a pouty voice. "That's the trouble. She's so ... so lifeless."

Mrs. Cravens came around the back of the trailer. "We wanted a calm horse—but not *this* calm."

"I've been taking riding lessons on Sugar at Dalton Stables for two months," Caroline complained. "Half the time I can't even get her to trot. The other kids there make fun of me. They call Sugar *The Ol' Gray Mare*, but they think it's my fault she's a plug."

I could feel Jake at my shoulder, but I didn't dare look up. "And she's gotten an okay from the vet?"

"Clean as a whistle," Mr. Cravens said. "That's why we're here. Ralph Dalton said he'd sell the mare for me, but Ray told us he knew someone who could work miracles with horses. I hope for Caroline's sake he's right."

I felt my stomach tighten and twist like drying leather. What if I couldn't help? Sure, I'd connected with different horses, bonded with them and figured out their problems. But I'd never done it as a job.

All I wanted now was for the humans to all go away and leave me with the horse. As nervous as I felt with everybody watching me, I was afraid I'd pass on my nerves to Sugar.

As if Jen had read my mind, she said, "Why don't I give you a tour of the place while Scoop unloads your horse?"

"Horsefeathers is a funny name for a stable," Caroline said as they headed into the barn. "Why do you call it Horsefeathers?"

"Why, *horsefeathers*, Caroline!" Jen said, laughing. "If you hang around Scoop for a while, you'll understand."

As soon as they moved to the paddock and were out of sight, I let down the trailer ramp. The gray mare didn't budge, even when the metal clanged and scraped on the gravel. "Horsefeathers," I mumbled. "There *is* such a thing as too calm, Sugar."

The mare's tail was clutched tight to her hocks, but there were no other signs of tension. She shifted her weight from side to side, but I sensed she did it from tiredness, not nervousness.

A car door slammed. Sugar didn't even twitch an ear. I peeked around the trailer. Maggie 37 came running up the lane, holding onto her red cowboy hat. She'd changed into red jeans and a red plaid shirt.

"Scoop!" she shouted, waving her free hand in the air. "Am I too late?" A white car sped off, spitting gravel behind. "Matthew's brother said he'd drop me off, but Matthew had to stop home first. Did I miss anything?"

I ignored her and climbed into the trailer with Sugar. The trailer smelled like Lysol and hay. "Hey, Sugar," I murmured, moving to the front and lowering my face close to hers. She didn't respond, but she didn't pull away. I blew gently into her nostrils, the way horses make themselves known to each other. But Sugar didn't blow back.

"Are you ready to come out of here, Sugar?" I asked. My mind flashed back to the day when I'd unloaded Carla's horse, Buckingham's British Pride. It was the day they moved to West Salem. "Ham," as we call him now, had almost overturned the trailer, he was so wound up.

But not Sugar. She didn't lift a hoof. I sensed that she wasn't being stubborn or strong-willed. She just didn't care enough to pick up her hooves.

I snapped on Sugar's lead rope and tugged until she stepped backwards down the ramp. At the end of the ramp, the mare just stood there, not even bothering to check out her new home.

"Scoop?" Maggie yelled. "Didn't you hear me?"

Sugar didn't flick an ear. Me either. I was still mad at Maggie for being so late.

"I'm glad I got here in time," Maggie said in her fake Texas accent. "I was afraid I'd miss them. How are they? Are they nice?"

"I needed you, Maggie," I said without looking at her. "You know I'm terrible talking to strangers. If Jen hadn't shown up, I don't know what I'd have done."

"Jen's here?" she asked, looking around for her. Without warning, Maggie switched into a British accent. "I am ever so sorry, Scoop! Scout's honor I am. I shall make it up to you. Forgive me, Love?"

Jen and everybody else came out of the barn. Maggie pivoted toward them. "Wow!" she whispered to me out of the side of her mouth. "Is that Ray's cousin from Kennsington? He's lovely, isn't he! And look there, Scoop. Blimey! He's sneaking looks at you—and he likes what he sees, I dare say."

"Stop it, Maggie," I whispered. My face felt like it was burning. I stroked Sugar's neck under her wavy, gray mane.

Maggie didn't wait to be introduced. She marched straight up to the Cravens and held out her hand to Mrs. Cravens. "Hello! I am Maggie 37 Red. Charmed, I'm sure." Maggie changes her last name as easily as she changes the colors of her clothes. She's always looking for the perfect stage name.

Maggie shook hands with Mr. Cravens, while Ray introduced her to his aunt and uncle.

"And you must be Caroline," Maggie said, bending down to look her in the eyes. "Would you like to learn a bit of trick riding while your horse is at Horsefeathers?"

"Sure!" Caroline said. You could tell that Maggie already had the younger girl in her spell. One more fan.

"And you're Jake," Maggie said, shaking his hand. "Where do you go to school, Jake? Ray didn't say."

"Kennsington High School—my first year," Jake said, smiling to reveal dimples and white teeth.

"Do you know Brad Gerwig?" Maggie asked. "He's a sophomore there."

"I don't think so," Jake said. "That school is so big, I hardly get to know anybody. We moved to Kennsington in the middle of the school year last year."

"It is *so* hard to make new friends," Maggie said dramatically, over-playing her role, if you ask me. Besides, Maggie 37 has never had trouble making new friends. People she hardly knows think they're her buddies.

"You know, Jake," Maggie said, cocking her head to the side. "We're having a mixer at our school to help kids get to know each other. You should come! Ray?" Maggie turned to him and slipped into her Southern accent. "Why don't y'all bring your cousin to our mixer?"

Ray shrugged. "I don't know if I'll come or not. I wanted to go with Carla, but she won't be back from Kentucky in time."

"Now, don't you worry about that. Y'all come!" Maggie drawled. "Scoop and Jen and I will take good care of y'all."

Maggie smiled back at me, and I wanted to go right through the ground. I didn't look at them. Instead, I pretended to be checking out Sugar's forelegs.

"Let's get going," Mr. Cravens said, moving toward the station wagon. "Thanks for the tour, Jen. We'll come out and check on Sugar Wednesday, if that's all right, Scoop."

They climbed in and drove off, the empty trailer bumping down the lane and stirring up dust. We stared after them.

"Well, I better go relieve Travis," Jen said, heading for her bike.

"Now that's a job I could handle," Maggie said. She's had a crush on Jen's brother for as long as I can remember.

"Thanks again for coming, Jen. I don't know what I would have done without you." I said it as much to slam Maggie as to thank Jen.

We watched Jen bike off down the lane, waving backwards at us.

"Don't be mad, Scoop," Maggie drawled, elbowing me gently. "Can I take Sugar here into the barn and brush her?" She rolled her big, brown cow eyes at me.

It's almost impossible to stay mad at Maggie 37. "Yeah, go on, Maggie. And take that silly red coat off of her," I said.

Sugar followed Maggie like an old dog. "She's so calm," Maggie said. "I don't think we'll have any trouble with this one, do you?"

"I don't know," I said. "The problem is she's *too* calm."

Maggie led Sugar into the barn. I needed to finish the chores and get home to help Dotty with Grandad. I scooped feed out of the bin and hurried around the side of the barn toward Ham's pasture.

Smack! I ran into something and spilled the coffee can full of grains all over the ground. I looked up, expecting to see Maggie. Instead, it was Stephen Dalton.

"Horsefeathers, Stephen! What are you doing here?" I yelled. "You're spying on us, aren't you!"

"I am not," he said.

"You were watching us get that mare, weren't you?" I accused. "You couldn't stand it that Horsefeathers Stable took one away from Dalton Stables!"

Maggie stepped out of the barn. "Why, if it isn't Stephen Dalton! Did you come by here to try to steal Sugar back? Too bad for you, Stevie. You're too late. Face it. It didn't work out for the poor horse at Dalton Stables. Be a man! Chalk one up for Horsefeathers."

Stephen smirked at us with thin, twisted lips that reminded me of worms. I expected him to look embarrassed or angry, but he didn't. He looked smug. And he wasn't faking it either.

"Boy, have you guys got it wrong," he said. "I came here to thank you for taking that creature off our hands. We were never so glad to get rid of a horse in all our lives."

An icy chill flicked down my spine. Something was very wrong with this picture. "What are you talking about, Stephen Dalton? What's wrong with that horse?"

Stephen chuckled from somewhere so low in his throat, his chest moved. "You'll see," he said. "You'll see."

5

Tuesday morning I was running late. Dotty seemed so caught up with Grandad she didn't notice that I skipped breakfast or that B.C. had locked himself in the bathroom and declared he'd never go back to school.

Grandad rocked in his rocking chair in the living room, the familiar *squeak, clunk* faster than usual. Dotty kneeled in front of him and stared up. I couldn't help but overhear as she talked back and forth from Grandad to God and back.

"Now Jared," she said in a voice she might have used on a little boy. "You know that you and me ain't never passed much in the way of words. So I don't have a mind for where you stand with the good Lord. Lord, help me understand. So I'm asking you, Jared, if you've gone and trusted Jesus to pay for your sins. 'Cause if you ain't, now's the time to confess them, say you're sorry, and then thank Him for dying for you so's you'll be forgiven. Thank You for raising from the dead, Lord, and for giving us all salvation. I reckon this is betwixt the two of you. Amen."

Grandad stared at the blank TV without blinking. I felt sorry for Dotty. I knew she worried about Grandad's faith. Sometimes I did too.

Dotty groaned as she got up off her knees. She tugged at her black slacks and tried to straighten her *Hi! I'm Dottie!* name tag.

I helped her. "When are you going to tell Mr. Ford to get you a name tag with your name spelled right?" I asked.

"I reckon it don't matter much," she said. She glanced around the room. "Where's B.C.?"

I sighed. "Bathroom. Good luck. I'm off."

Grandad didn't move when I told him good-bye. His bony arms rested on the arms of the rocker. I put my hand on his, and it felt cold and stiff. "See you tonight, Grandad," I said.

Outside the sky was streaked with pink. I remembered something Grandad used to say: "Red skies at night—sailors' delight. Red skies at morning—sailors take warning." If the saying held for land, we might be in for some bad weather.

Orphan nickered and met me at the fence. Every time I see her, I get a strong feeling inside of me that makes me want to pray. It's like a yank out of the worst parts of the world and into something real, where God is bigger and I'm smaller but more peaceful.

I didn't see Sugar in the pasture with the other horses. Even Dogless was outside, curled up on Ham's broad back. Lines of dust striped the inside of the barn where sunlight squeezed through the cracks. Sugar stood in her stall in almost the exact position I'd left her in the night before.

I entered the stall with her. "Morning, Sugar," I said. She paid no mind to me. Her head drooped, and her neck hung low. Something about her stall wasn't right. At first I couldn't place it. Then I saw the problem. Her stall door had been gnawed. More than gnawed. Sugar had eaten about two inches into the wood.

"Horsefeathers! So that's why the Daltons were so glad to get rid of you," I said. Cribbing, or crib-biting, can wreck a stall. "Why did you stay in here all night, Sugar?"

Sugar shifted her weight from one foot to the other. I took her by the halter and led her out into the paddock. She didn't try to resist me. Her hooves shuffled, kicking up dust as we walked. I fed her outside and hurried through the rest of my chores while she ate. I hated school for keeping me from a morning ride on Orphan.

Before I left, I turned Sugar out in the south pasture, away from the stall. Maybe Jen had read of cures for cribbing. I knew that swallowing the wood wasn't the worst danger. Horses that crib or chew wood usually run a greater risk from swallowing air. "Wind-sucking" bloats the stomach and messes up digestion. Fixing Sugar was looking like a tougher job all the time.

I had to run to school. By the time I got there, Maggie and Jen had already gone in. The halls were strung with streamers. Signs on the lockers announced: *Freshman Mixer! Friday at 8:00!*

Maggie ran up to me. She looked like an exotic tree, with her green overalls, green turtleneck, and green headband. "Scoop! Isn't it cool? I can't wait for Friday!"

Ray sauntered up the hall. "Maggie 37 Green!" he called. "How come you're keeping this mixer such a secret?"

"You better be there, Ray!" Maggie said. "And bring that cute cousin of yours too!"

"Caroline?" Ray asked, brown eyes twinkling.

"No, silly!" Maggie said in an unidentified accent. "Jake!"

"You think Jake's cute?" Ray asked. "And he thinks Scoop is cute. What's the world coming to?"

I sneaked a look at Ray to see if he was just teasing me. I didn't think so.

"Told you, Scoop," Maggie said before

being pulled away by a couple of guys. She hollered back at us over her shoulder as they hustled her down the hall. "I can always tell what's in a man's heart."

"*That Scoop is pretty cute,*" Ray said, mimicking Jake's deeper voice.

I looked up. "He did not say that, Ray," I said. No way any guy that cute himself would think I was cute. Ray had to be making it up. But what if he wasn't?

~~~~~~~~~~~~~~~~~~~~~~~~~~~~~~~~

All through morning classes I couldn't get that conversation out of my head. Jake Cravens— who was good-looking by anybody's standards— might actually have thought I was cute. He'd used the word *pretty* at Horsefeathers. I'd heard him with my own two ears. He'd said, *Why didn't you tell me Scoop was so pretty, Ray?*

All of a sudden I felt as if I had no idea what I looked like, as if I wouldn't have been able to pick myself out of a police lineup. I knew I wasn't ugly. I didn't have to worry about being too fat or too skinny, and there wasn't any part of my face I especially hated. But pretty? No way.

Still ... *That Scoop is pretty cute.* I could almost hear the words whispered in my ear, louder than the banging of lunch trays, the clanging of silverware, the shouts across the cafeteria.

I gobbled down lunch, then did something I almost never do. I ventured into the girls' restroom. Most of the time I'd rather explode than go in there and fight for a toilet or a sink. Cackles echoed off the sewer-green concrete walls in outbursts, like popping firecrackers. I pushed my way through to the mirror, ending up in the middle, where a crack ran jagged from bottom to top.

"Scoop, what are you doing here?" Maggie Green was braiding her hair to fall to the side, in front of her left shoulder. "Are you sick?"

"Just washing my hands," I said. I turned on the water and sneaked a look at myself. My own reflection startled me. I looked almost as tall as Maggie, and my face seemed clear and zit-free, as if I'd never had a pimple in my whole life. My hair was messy, but it looked good long, and I liked the way it had parted to the side all by itself. I stood up straight. The rest of me didn't look half bad. I'd either lost weight or it shifted to the right places over the summer.

That Scoop is pretty cute. Maybe Ray really was telling the truth. Maybe Jake actually thought I was cute. And maybe all changes weren't so bad after all.

~~~~~~~~~~~~~~~~~~~~~~~~~~~~~

I worked hard with Sugar after school. I even cut my ride on Orphan short so I could try

48

Sugar again. I practiced the mare on the lunge line, a long rein that looks like a super-long ribbon. I stood in the middle and made the horse move in a large circle around me. But I couldn't get the "old gray mare" to do anything more than a slow walk. Even cracking the whip in the dirt behind her didn't phase her. She just didn't care. No wonder the Cravens had gotten fed up with her.

They'd be coming out to visit Sugar on Wednesday, and so far I had nothing to show them except a chewed-up stall. Sugar had eaten her grain from the middle of the feed bucket, but left the grain at the corners, as if nosing around to get it all would have required too much effort from her. No matter what I did with that mare, her heart wasn't in it. I checked her teeth to make sure she wasn't older than they thought she was when they bought her at auction. The groove on her incisor, the Galvayne's Groove, came down a little more than halfway, which would make her around 15 years old, the same age they said she was. So the problem wasn't her age. She should have been in her prime.

I gave up for the day and put Sugar out to pasture with Orphan, hoping some of my horse would rub off on her.

By the time I got home, Dotty's car was already parked in the driveway. I stepped onto the porch and heard a *clink, plunk* behind me.

Two bottle caps hit the step. A dozen or so more bottle caps lay scattered across the skinny porch planks.

I looked up on the roof for B.C. "How was school, B.C.?" I hollered up, spotting a shadow almost to the peak.

"I hate school!" he cried, dumping a shower of bottle caps. They rolled down the roof and fell like a metal waterfall to the porch.

I covered my head and dodged as best I could. "Stop it, B.C.!" I screamed.

For B.C. to be flinging his beloved bottle caps, I knew it had to be bad. Our dad used to work in the bottle cap plant on the outskirts of town. Every night after his shift, he'd bring B.C. a pocketful of bottle caps. Even though it had been more than seven years since our parents died in a plant explosion, B.C. still had most of his bottle caps. Some kids had security blankets. My brother had security bottle caps.

B.C. climbed down, and I helped him pick up the caps he'd dropped on me and the porch. His eyes looked red, and his nose was runny.

"I'm not going back to school," he said. "Teacher said I can't bring bottle caps to school anymore."

I suspected there was a big chunk of the story my brother was leaving out, but I wasn't sure I wanted to hear it. "You can have the bottle caps here waiting for you," I said. "I think it's probably a good idea anyway—to leave them at home."

"Fine," he said, "because I'm not going to school ever again."

Dotty had the table set when we walked in. The kitchen smelled like cold pork 'n' beans. Grandad sat at the head of the table holding a fistful of spoons, which were suspiciously absent from everybody else's place setting.

My aunt didn't seem to hear us over the running water at the kitchen sink. Her back was to us, and she kept talking: "Jared, Jesus loved you so much He died for you." She was still at it. Nobody would ever accuse Dotty of being a quitter.

"Well, if it ain't my two sunshines!" Dotty said turning from the sink and wiping her hands on the dish towel.

Grandad hardly ate anything for supper, and B.C. ate everything. After supper, Grandad wouldn't let go of the mayonnaise jar. Dotty wanted to put it away. In the end, she gave in and let him take the jar to bed with him.

I was so tired I went up to bed early and almost fell asleep reading our world history chapter. I closed the book and huddled under the blankets in my little attic room that's shaped like the letter A. The horsefeather Carla had given me sat on my desk. Actually, it was the feather of a cuckoo bird. Carla told me that cuckoo birds end up in adopted families, like me. They might feel as out of place as a feather on a horse sometimes, but they end up where they belong.

I stared out the window and imagined folding up God's world—the stars, my room, the dresser, the bed, the horsefeather, and me. Then I prayed and gave everything back to God, including Little Sugar General.

The next day the Cravens would come to Horsefeathers to check on their horse, and I hadn't made a speck of progress. As I drifted to sleep, images floated through my head like heat waves—Mrs. Cravens saying, "We didn't think you would be *this* young." Caroline saying, "If you can't fix her, we have to sell her." And Jake saying, "That Scoop is pretty cute."

6

On Wednesday morning, I got up before Dotty—a landmark in our house. My aunt had brought home two sweaters from our church's rummage sale in July, and I hadn't worn either of them. I found them in a brown bag under my bed.

In the bathroom I tried on both sweaters, standing on my tiptoes to try to see myself in the medicine cabinet mirror. Finally I settled on the turquoise, short-sleeved sweater that looked new. I pulled on an almost-new pair of jeans and spent a little extra time trying to figure out how to get my hair to stay parted to the side.

As soon as Horsefeathers came into view, I realized something was wrong. Orphan whinnied and paced the fence. I ran to the paddock and found Sugar. She was weaving, shifting her weight from one foreleg to the other, her head and neck swinging from side to side like the pendulum in Grandad's old grandfather clock.

I froze, looking on in horror as she threw herself back and forth like a drunken cow. If she kept that up, she'd wreck her knees. No wonder Stephen Dalton had acted so smug. Weaving was an even harder habit to break than cribbing.

I tried giving Sugar half of the apple I'd brought for Orphan. But when I held it out to her, the mare wouldn't even sniff it. She looked like she was in a trance. Why couldn't I figure out what was wrong?

Lord, I prayed, *I'm stumped here. Please show me what's wrong with this horse.*

I had time for a quick ride on Orphan if I didn't take time to bridle her. I needed that ride, needed to fly with my own horse and shake off everything else.

I didn't want to get horsehairs all over my new sweater, but my nylon jacket covered most of it. I swung myself up on Orphan and settled onto her soft, firm back. Then I let her take me around the pasture at a canter. Colors raced by, blues swirling into greens, dotted with orange and red streaks.

One, two, three, float. When all four legs leave the ground on that fourth beat of a canter, it feels like Orphan and I are flying. I needed to fly.

We sped up to a gallop. Every worry I had about the Cravens coming to Horsefeathers that afternoon drained out of me, whisked away by the wind. Why couldn't every minute of life be just like this—pure joy without any problems?

What if we just got God's best parts to life, without all the bad stuff that happens in between the good—sickness, death, explosions?

Orphan trotted back to the barn. I finished chores, tried unsuccessfully to get Sugar's attention, then left for school, brushing horse hairs off my new jeans and trying to smooth down my hair.

~~~~~~~~~~~~~~~~~~~~~~~~~~~~~~~

"So how goes it with the Cravens' nag?" Stephen asked. He'd plopped into the empty seat next to me in our last-hour class. "I'm telling you, things have really gotten better at Dalton Stables since we got rid of that nag. Do you know what she did? Besides chewing through three stall doors, she kicked one whole wall in. So, Scoop the famous horse woman, have you cured that old gray mare yet?"

I didn't answer him, but fished out my language arts book from my backpack. I sure hoped Sugar didn't kick in our walls.

"Sorry?" he said. "I couldn't hear your answer."

I ignored him.

"What are you all dressed up for anyway?" Stephen asked.

"I'm not dressed up," I said, dropping the book in my lap and digging into my pack for a pen.

Stephen shrugged and slumped in his seat. "I hate this class," he whispered. "It's stupid."

We'd been assigned a short story by O. Henry, and it was actually pretty interesting hearing Ms. Whitmore tell us what it meant. But all during class Stephen sighed and squirmed and stared at his watch.

Something dropped on the floor between Stephen and me. Without thinking, I leaned over and picked it up. "Yuck!" I said, dropping it as fast as if it had been on fire. It was Stephen's pencil, slimy and gross with teeth marks all over it. The eraser had been gnawed off. He'd been chewing and slobbering until the gold paint had flecked away.

Ms. Whitmore gave me a dirty look, then turned to write our assignment on the board.

"That is so gross, Stephen!" I whispered, a quiver of disgust shaking through me. "Why do you chew on your pencil like that?"

"Because I'm bored out of my gourd!" he said. "This class is boring! What else is there to do?"

Then the thought struck me like a good swift horse's kick. "Horsefeathers!" I said. "That's it!"

"Scoop?" Ms. Whitmore said. "Did you just have some kind of revelation you'd like to share with the rest of us?"

"I'm sorry, Ms. Whitmore," I said. But she

was right. I had gotten a revelation. I knew what was wrong with Sugar. The poor horse was bored out of her gourd. What could be more boring than a solitary stall at Dalton Stables? Locked up in that small, white box 22 hours a day? Who wouldn't go nuts? Who wouldn't start chewing wood just for something to do? Stephen chewed his pencil; Sugar chewed her stall.

Horsefeathers! I had the answer to Sugar's problem. And I had Stephen Dalton and his chewed-up pencil to thank for it!

~~~~~~~~~~~~~~~~~~~~~~~~~~~~

After class I looked for Jen. I knew Maggie had to meet with her committee to plan Friday's mixer, so she couldn't face the Cravens with me. But good ol' Travis Zucker had not only volunteered to cover for Jen again, he'd offered to give both of us a ride to the barn.

I found Jen right away. But we had to wait so long for Travis I was afraid he'd forgotten about us. Finally I spotted his white pickup as it pulled around the corner and onto the curb.

Jen slid in first and scooted next to her brother. I hopped in next to her. Travis leaned forward and smiled over at me. "You look nice, Scoop," he said. He laughed softly. "Yep, you clean up real good."

I felt my face heat up and was glad Travis couldn't see me blush. "Thanks a lot," I said.

Definitely a Palomino stallion. It was easy to see why Maggie had such a crush on him. "Seriously, Travis," I managed to say as he pulled off the curb with a *bump, bump,* "thanks for the ride to Horsefeathers."

"No problem. I imagine I'll find a way to get even with Jen, right, Sis?"

"I suppose," she said, her mouth struggling not to turn up into a grin.

The Zuckers are such a nice family that sometimes it hurts to be around them. I can't help imagining what it would be like to have a regular family like that. Sometimes I feel bad because I can't remember much about my mom and dad. I worry that their faces are fading from my brain. But other times a memory flashes back so sharp it could have happened yesterday.

I was anxious to see what Jen thought of my bored horse theory. "Listen you guys," I said. "I think I know what's wrong with Sugar."

"That the new horse Ray brought over?" Travis asked.

I nodded. "I got the idea when I saw Stephen chewing his pencil in English class."

Jen frowned back at me. "Scoop? Are you all right?"

The truck hit a bump, and Travis turned into Horsefeathers' lane.

"Listen," I pleaded. "Stephen gnaws on his pencil because he's bored. That's why I think

Sugar chews on wood too! Maybe that's all that's wrong with her. She's shell-shocked bored from being cooped up at Dalton Stables. And if we can get her over being bored, maybe we can cure her. What do you think?"

Jen's blond eyebrows came together above her nose, and I could almost hear her brain sizzle. "Dalton Stables is pretty boring all right," she said.

"Looks like Ray's relatives beat you here," Travis said, pulling the truck to a stop. "Sorry."

A blue Volvo sat under the oak tree by the barn. In the paddock, Caroline and her mother were standing by Sugar.

"They can't be here yet!" I cried. "I was hoping to try out a couple of my ideas on Sugar before they got here." I wanted to have something good to report.

The disappointment inside me was so strong I wasn't sure if I was upset because the Cravens had come too early or because only Caroline and her mother had come. Jake was nowhere in sight.

7

We hopped out of the pickup and thanked Travis before he drove away.

I walked to the paddock and climbed the fence as Orphan trotted up. Orphan's neck arched and she playfully tossed her head at me, begging for a ride or a game.

Sugar hadn't budged. Her neck drooped low, and her tail sagged at her hocks.

"They're here!" Caroline yelled, running up to me. "Is Sugar doing better? Did you fix her?"

"Not yet," I admitted.

"The mare doesn't seem any better," said Mrs. Cravens. "She was weaving side to side like she was drunk when we drove up. Ralph Dalton had his grooms fit her with an anti-weaving grill. Shouldn't she be wearing one now?"

I'd seen anti-weaving contraptions before — rigged to poke the horse when he moved sideways. "They don't work, Mrs. Cravens—unless you want your horse to wear that thing every minute of the day. I wouldn't want Sugar to have to go through that again. I have some other ideas I'd rather try. I think if we—"

"Where's her stable blanket?" Mrs. Cravens interrupted, as if she'd just now noticed Sugar wasn't wearing it. "Did that horse tear the blanket off again? She did that at Dalton Stables too."

"Not exactly," I said. Why couldn't I just be left alone to take care of the horses? I looked around for Jen to help. She hadn't budged from her spot on the other side of the paddock fence. Coward.

I took a deep breath and prayed God would help me know what to say. "At Horsefeathers Stable we don't like to mess up the way horses are naturally, the way God made them."

"What?" Mrs. Cravens narrowed her eyes and gave me a look that showed I wasn't exactly scoring points in the confidence department.

I tried again. "Horses will grow their own blankets as the weather gets cooler if we don't mess up the way nature works. And their coats will be a hundred times better than any kind of stable blanket. But if we blanket them, their own coats won't grow right and they'll end up without their fur when they need it."

"She'll look like a wooly sheep though, won't she?" Mrs. Craven's asked. "Ralph Dalton said the blanket would preserve her show coat ... not that we'll ever get this nag into a show ring."

She glared at Sugar while Caroline snapped her fingers in front of her horse, trying in vain to get her to come to life.

"She'll lose her furry coat by show season," I explained. "Besides—"

A voice from the barn called out, "Did Sugar do this?"

I turned to see Jake standing in the door of Sugar's stall. Something weird clogged my throat and I had to swallow before I could say anything. Jake walked toward us, grinning as a hello.

I tried to smile back.

"Did Caroline's horse chew your barn to pieces?" he asked again.

"Um ... yeah, Sugar did bite her crib," I said, clearing my throat to get rid of my wimpy, crackling voice.

Jake turned to his sister. "Caroline, are you sure you didn't buy a giant, gray woodpecker by mistake?"

She chased after him, swatting the air as he dodged away.

"I know you mean well, Scoop," Mrs. Cravens said, not taking her eyes off Sugar.

Here it comes. She's going to fire me. She's giving up on Horsefeathers without giving us a chance. She gave the Daltons two months. I get two days.

Mrs. Cravens didn't look at me. "Caroline's father and I, we've been talking it over, what's best for Caroline. And well, maybe we made a mistake coming here."

"*Yeeehaa!*" The holler came from the pasture.

We turned to see a streak of white tear across the green grass, jump the fence into the paddock, and run straight for us. Maggie 37 White, dressed in her new color from her white hat to her white boots, galloped a circle around us on her trusty white horse Moby.

Jen climbed the fence and joined us in the center of the ring just as Moby stopped on a dime, inches from the immovable Sugar. Moby reared high, her forelegs pawing the air, while Maggie waved her hat high above her. Moby went from a rear to a low bow, and Maggie drew her hat across her heart. They took off again, and Maggie got to her feet in the saddle, standing in it as Moby cantered around the paddock ring.

"Yea!" cried Caroline. "That's great!"

"Not bad!" Jake said.

I sneaked a glance at Mrs. Cravens, and she looked pretty impressed too.

Maggie slid off Moby and led her to us. Sugar hadn't so much as lifted a hoof during the whole performance.

"Wow!" Caroline exclaimed, stroking Moby. "Can you teach me how to do that?"

Caroline's mother laughed. "I can't imagine your mare ever doing that, Honey." She shook her head, then sang, "*The old gray mare, she ain't what she used to be.* I guess we should have gotten you a younger horse."

"Why, excuse me, Ma'am," Maggie said in her Texas cowgirl accent. "Moby here is 23 years old, pushing 24. That would make Sugar a young whipper-snapper."

Whipper-snapper? Where did she come up with these things? I had to grin, and though I didn't aim it at anybody in particular, Jake was grinning my way and we sort of exchanged grins.

Maggie kept up the cowgirl charm, turning it on Caroline. "And as for you, Little Miss, we'll have you trick riding in no time!"

Mrs. Cravens laughed, and the whole atmosphere changed. After five minutes with Maggie 37, and five minutes of Caroline begging to keep Sugar at Horsefeathers, Mrs. Cravens caved. Maggie had saved the day and bought me some time. Mrs. Cravens even agreed to give me a couple of days to work with Sugar before they checked back at Horsefeathers.

Jen and Maggie and I walked the Cravens to their car. Jake was the last one to get in.

"So Jake," Maggie said, "you and Ray *are* coming to the mixer Friday night, right?"

"This Friday?" he asked.

"Yes, this Friday," Maggie said. "Why don't you guys go together? Jen and Scoop and you and Ray?"

If Maggie's leg had been under a table, I

would have kicked it. All I could do was stare at my feet and feel like I was going to die.

"Huh? Okay." He said it like it was no big deal. Like he'd said okay to Coke instead of Pepsi.

My heart was pounding so hard in my ears that at first I didn't hear Mrs. Cravens. Maggie pushed me closer to the driver's window and followed me there as Jake got in the backseat.

"Excuse me?" Maggie said to her. "I couldn't quite hear you."

"I was just asking what you thought the odds were of this horse working out. I don't mean to sound rude, but I really can't see any progress at all yet. Do you still think Scoop can cure our horse?" She was asking Maggie now. At least she had confidence in one of us.

"Do I think Scoop can cure Sugar? Absolutely!" Maggie declared. "Money back guarantee!"

"Oh is that right?" Mrs. Cravens said. "Money back guarantee? That's wonderful. Ray didn't say anything about that."

I heard Jen gasp. Mrs. Cravens started the engine.

I stared at Maggie, my mouth hanging open. We didn't have a money back guarantee! In fact, I'd already used some of Mrs. Cravens' money to order feed.

They left in a cloud of dust. As soon as they

were out of earshot, Jen turned on Maggie. "Maggie 37 White! What were you thinking? We can't afford to give their money back! Now what are we going to do?"

We glared at Maggie, but she seemed totally unaffected by it. "Oh don't worry about it," she said. "You have a mixer to think about. We better figure out what you're going to wear."

8

Maggie and Jen left Horsefeathers for the Zucker house to try to get something together for Jen to wear to the mixer. I couldn't even let myself think about that or what on earth *I'd* find to wear. Right now, I had to think about Sugar—and Maggie's moneyback guarantee.

Dogless Cat hung out with Buckingham's British Pride and kept away from the gray mare while I brushed her. I whistled for Orphan and convinced her to hang around with Sugar and me.

Instead of giving Sugar her afternoon feed, I decided to vary her routine. I doled out a handful of grain every 15 minutes, making her move to a new spot each time—in the center of the paddock, in the pasture, down by the pond, back to the stallway inside the barn. I was going to entertain that horse if she appreciated it or not. And so far, she did *not*.

Next, I hooked a long lead rope to Sugar's halter and led her to the south pasture. I called Orphan, and she trotted up, tossing her head playfully. "Let's take this mare for a ride, Orphan," I said.

Orphan held still while I swung up on her back. "Okay, Girl! You lead, we'll follow."

Orphan started at a walk toward the stream. At first, I was afraid Sugar would balk. I turned and coaxed her, "Come on, Sugar. Follow the leader!"

The mare shuffled after Orphan, her head hung low and her eyes glassy as I tugged on her lead rope. At the stream, Orphan splashed through and stopped in the middle, taking time out for a cool drink. The water looked so clear and refreshing I could have sipped it myself. But Sugar might as well have been standing on the banks of a sand dune. She didn't even look down.

We headed back to Horsefeathers. Orphan and I got Sugar to walk a bit faster, but she wouldn't break into a trot no matter what I tried. As we got closer to the barn, I heard a methodical *thump, thump, thump*. Then I spotted B.C. in the paddock, throwing a tennis ball against the barn. He missed catching it and scrambled in the dirt after the fuzzy, green ball.

"B.C.!" I hollered, and waved. He waved back. I felt bad that I hadn't taken the time to find out how he was really getting along in school. They almost hadn't graduated him to fourth grade. He's smart enough, but when he's in the manic part of his manic depression, he can disrupt his whole class without even knowing it. And when he's in the depressed part of manic depression, he has trouble getting his work done.

B.C. stopped playing ball and came over when I slid off Orphan. "Why are you leading that gray horse, Scoop?" he asked. "Can I ride her? Or can I ride Orphan? You never let me ride Orphan. I'm a good rider too. Really, really good. I'm as good a rider as you. You should let me help out at Horsefeathers more. What's wrong with this horse? What's her name? How old is she?"

He said it all almost before I hit the ground. It didn't take a genius to figure out B.C.'s mood had swung to manic.

"Slow down, B.C.," I said. "This is Sugar, and I think that the only thing wrong with her is that she's bored. If you want to, you can lead her into the barn with me." I scruffed his bushy, brown hair that stuck out all over like a weed patch.

"Gimme, gimme!" He grabbed the rope out of my hand and jerked it.

"Careful, B.C.," I said, leading Orphan in beside Sugar. "Hook her to the cross-ties while I brush Orphan."

My horse wasn't even warm, so it didn't take much to cool her and brush her down.

Sugar was standing quietly in the cross-ties, but at first I didn't see B.C. He was at the far end of the stallway, fiddling with an old saddle. I'd set out the Western saddle so I could clean it up with saddle soap, but I never seem to get to it.

"B.C.? You want to get the brushes?" I knew he couldn't concentrate. He never can when he gets like that. I had a feeling his new teacher may have gotten a full dose of B.C. that day. I wondered how she'd handled it.

"Huh?" B.C. asked, wrinkling up his whole face so he looked like Grandad. "Oh yeah."

I brushed Sugar with Orphan's brush while I waited for B.C. And waited. And waited. "B.C.?" I hollered, when I'd almost finished brushing the mare. "Where'd you go?"

My brother didn't answer, but I heard him singing on the roof. It sounded like "Grandad Got Run over by a Reindeer."

Before feeding Sugar a little in her stall, I decided to brighten things up for her a bit. I hung her red stable blanket over one wall to give her something cheerful to look at if she kept to her stall. The horses always have water available from the stream or the pond, but I filled a bright green plastic bucket with water and set it in her stall for fun.

Next, I filled a net bag with hay and hung it from the wall. I poured some oats in a jug and dangled it from the ceiling, poking a small hole in the plastic so a little oats would leak out if Sugar got ambitious enough to bump it with her nose.

"Now you're all set if you feel like playing in here," I told Sugar as I turned her loose in her stall. Her ears pricked up and moved like antennae for the first time since she'd arrived at Horsefeathers. And her eyes looked different too—less glassy. "And if you want to play outside, Orphan says she'll be happy to oblige."

"Now for my brother," I said out loud. *Lord, help me help B.C.*

I climbed to the barn roof and found B.C. trying to hammer down shingles with his bare fist. "Thanks, B.C.," I said. "Come and sit with me a minute before we go home, will you? I need to ask your advice on something."

"You know," B.C. said, pounding his fist on another nail, "I could come back here after supper and take care of this whole roof. Tommy Zucker says he has his own toolbox. He told Jimmy Mitchell, not me. But I heard. But I don't think he really does have his own toolbox. He just told Jimmy that. Jimmy isn't very nice at recess. He didn't want me to play ball on his team today, but I'm really good this year. I can hit a home run if they let me bat."

I motioned for him to come and sit, and he

whizzed over and plopped down beside me. He picked at shingles and pulled them up as he talked. "I like that horse down there. She seems really nice. Are they paying you a lot of money to ride her?"

"I hope so," I said. "B.C., tell me about school. How do you like fourth grade so far?"

"I don't like any of the girls. Tommy Zucker likes this girl Stephanie something. And Jimmy likes her too."

"But are things going okay?" I asked. I put my arm on his shoulder and could feel his little muscles twitch.

"Sometimes I don't know what my teacher is saying. Like directions. I messed up today. I don't think she likes me already." He'd pulled one whole shingle off the roof, but I was afraid to stop him, afraid he'd jump subjects again.

"I'll bet your teacher likes you okay, B.C.," I said, although I wasn't sure about that. "They just ... they don't always understand what it's like being B.C. Teachers don't always understand me either, what it's like being Scoop." That was true enough, and not just about teachers either. "So it's a good thing God understands us, huh B.C.?"

B.C. looked me square in the eyes. "What's wrong with me again? I was going to tell Jimmy what it's called. *Man depression*? Is that it?"

I swallowed hard. "Manic depression. You almost had it. I'll bet Jimmy and Tommy don't know that word. You're a smart kid, B.C."

"Yeah," he said. "Let's go."

Sometimes I wish I could freeze B.C.'s good moods and junk the bad ones, but Dotty says life is a package deal. All of B.C.'s moods are part of the B.C. package.

We walked home together. B.C. talked about a million things. But a couple of them were pretty good. When I told him Sugar was bored, he said we should play ball with her or volleyball. And he said he'd bring his radio to the barn next time.

We were late for supper, but Dotty and Grandad hadn't gotten to it anyway.

"You're home!" Dotty cried as soon as we set foot in the house. "B.C., you gotta leave me a note when you take off like that! Scoop, see to that mess over by the fridge, will ya? Mrs. Powers from church called—"

"The Hat Lady?" B.C. asked. That's what B.C. calls her because she sits in front of us in church and wears big hats every Sunday.

"Yes, B.C., Honey. Go wash your hands. So she calls me at work when she stops by to check on your grandad. And she says 'Don't worry, Dotty. Jared's fine. But I think he's eating mustard.' Come to find out he ain't eating it. He's

73

scooping it behind the waste basket and taking the empty jar. I got him settled and cleaned up."

I wiped up the hardened yellow mustard while Dotty unwrapped cold cuts from white paper. I set out the applesauce and ketchup bottle. No mustard. We'd sat down to sandwiches and B.C.'s chatter about hummingbirds and his birthday next year, when I heard somebody knocking at the front door.

"I'll get it," I said, glad to leave the table.

Jen Zucker stood at the front door. She held a big grocery bag out to me. "Hi, Scoop!" Her blond hair hung down in soft curls.

"I like your hair," I said, taking the bag.

"Really?" she asked, tugging at one of the curls. "Maggie did it." She pointed to the pickup, where Maggie sat next to Travis. "She thinks I should wear it like this to the mixer. What do you think?"

"She's right," I said. Jen has a unique kind of beauty that her wire-rimmed glasses frame, making her look wise.

She turned to go, then came back. "Oh, the sack is stuff I made for Sugar." I felt through the sack as she talked. "There are apple roses, granola balls, carrot muffins, applesauce squares, and carrot crispies. Tomorrow I'll try to do corn clusters and haystack candy—out of molasses and real hay."

"What a great idea!" I said. Everything looked so good I could have eaten it myself. "Thanks, Jen."

Jen turned to go again, then came back. "Scoop, Maggie made me call Ray about the mixer. And his cousin was over."

"You called them?" I couldn't imagine calling them. I wouldn't have been able to talk. Maybe to Ray, but not to Jake. "What did they say?"

"They said Ray's uncle had to come to town to help Ray's dad with something. So he offered to drop the guys off at the mixer. And they're picking us up at my house at 7:45." Jen blushed.

"You're kidding!" I said, my stomach suddenly feeling like a herd of mustangs were running in it. "It's not ... a date or anything, is it?"

"Of course not!" Jen said. "You know my dad. He says I can't date until I'm 31. They're just giving us a ride. That's all." Jen's dad might say that, but I knew he couldn't say no to his daughter if she really wanted something.

"Sure," I said, trying to sound like it was nothing—Coke instead of Pepsi. Just two kids giving two more kids a ride to the mixer. That's all. "Yeah, thanks. I'll check with Dotty, but that sounds fine. I mean, a ride is good."

Jen hopped off the porch, her curls swinging as she strode to the truck. Maggie waved and

Travis honked as they drove off. I went back inside and showed Dotty and B.C. the horse treats Jen made. Something told me to hide them from Grandad though. Then, as nonchalantly as I could, I ran the mixer idea past Dotty. "And Jen said Ray's uncle is dropping Ray and Jake off at the school and they could pick us up too, if I can get to Jen's in time." I didn't look at her, but kept wiping the counter.

"That's nice," Dotty said, looking for something, opening the junk drawer and rifling through it. "Tell him thanks for me. I wouldn't want to leave Grandad and B.C. home alone."

Thank You, Lord, I prayed. Although it wasn't a big deal. And it wasn't a date. It was just a ride.

9

I could hardly wait until Thursday morning to try out Jen's horse treats on Sugar. B.C. seemed kind of quiet, which was okay by me. Grandad hadn't come out of his room, although we heard him talking to himself and wheezing a little. Dotty had most of the day covered with the Hat Lady and two of her friends from church who offered to take turns checking in on Grandad.

I finally settled on a few apple roses, an apple-sauce square, and one carrot crispie for Sugar's breakfast treat. Together they smelled like apple pie and made me so hungry I grabbed an apple for myself. Then I stuffed some of Jen's horse granola bars in my backpack for after school and hurried to Horsefeathers.

Orphan smells me or hears me coming long before I see her. She's always waiting in the pad-dock, her head over the fence. "Hey, Girl," I said, patting her gorgeous head. "How's our client this morning?" I sneaked my horse one apple rose.

Sugar was out in the near pasture grazing not far from Moby. A good sign. I said a silent prayer of thanks. When I walked out to her, Sugar lifted her head and looked directly at me.

"Hey there, Sugar!" I called. "Got something for you."

Sugar's ears pricked straight up for me. Then she walked up to meet me halfway. She was definitely coming out of her boredom. I could hardly believe how fast. The mare gratefully downed the rest of the apple roses and followed me to the barn. In between grooming, picking out horses' hooves, feeding, and mucking stalls, I doled out the rest of Jen's horse treats to Sugar.

~~~~~~~~~~~~~~~~~~~~~~~~~~~~~~~

I got to school before the first bell rang. Ray and Maggie were talking in front of math class. I filled them in on the good news about Sugar's progress. I felt better about the mixer and about Jake too. At least now I'd have something good to report about his sister's horse.

Stephen Dalton sat next to me in language arts again. As soon as he took out his pencil and put it between his teeth, I had to fight to keep from laughing. If he only knew that he was the one who gave me the solution to the bored horse problem!

"What's so funny?" he whispered.

I shook my head and pressed my lips together and almost choked myself to hold it in.

"What?" he asked. Stephen sniffed the air. "I smell cookies!" He sniffed closer to my backpack. "Or cake or something! You're sneaking food into class and I'm going to tell unless you give me some."

This time I did let out a chortle and got a dirty look from Ms. Whitmore, who looks kind of like Ethel Mertz, Lucy and Desi's neighbor in the old "I Love Lucy" reruns Dotty used to watch with B.C.

"You want some?" I asked Stephen, wondering what exactly Jen had put in her horse granola bars and if raw oats would do any permanent damage to humans.

Stephen stuck out his hand, facing Ms. Whitmore and glancing to the side at me. "Yeah! Give!" he whispered.

While I was trying to decide whether or not I'd give a horse treat to Stephen, the loud speaker screeched. The class groaned at the high-pitched noise that sounded like long fingernails scraping the blackboard.

"*Um ... I need Sarah Coop in the office. Will Sarah Coop come to the office, please?*" asked the voice of the principal, Mrs. Dorr.

"Ooooh, Sarah, what did you do this time?" Stephen asked, loud enough for the whole room to hear.

Several of the kids turned around and stared at me. Half of them probably didn't know who Sarah Coop was.

"Go ahead," Ms. Whitmore said, jotting something on her pad of hall passes.

I collected my pack, got up, and walked to the front of the room without a glance at anybody. My heart pounded in my ears as I took the pass and left the room. Behind me I heard Ms. Whitmore start talking again.

The hall was empty and made my walk to the principal's office seem scarier. I tried to remember if I'd done anything that might have gotten me in trouble, but I couldn't think of a thing. This was only our fourth day of high school. What could I have done already?

I peeked in the office, and the secretary frowned up at me from her computer.

"I'm Scoop," I said. "Sarah Coop?"

She didn't budge.

"The principal called me ... I mean, called for me on the intercom?"

She pointed to the principal's private office. "Go on in. You had a phone call."

A phone call? Immediately I thought of B.C. Something had happened to B.C. I should have talked to him at breakfast. If something had happened to him, I'd never forgive myself.

Principal Dorr motioned me into her office, a tiny room with just enough space for her desk and a chair on both sides of it. "Sarah, sorry to get you out of class. Your aunt called. She needs you to ..." She squinted at a piece of paper in her hand. I couldn't breathe. "She wants you to go find your grandfather. She's going home, I guess. And you're to go to the barn. Does that make sense?"

I exhaled. It wasn't B.C. He was probably still at school. "Yes," I said, taking the note from her. "Thank you. Can I go now?"

"Take your things with you," said Principal Dorr. "School's out in 20 minutes. Will you be all right? Do you need any help?"

"No thanks," I said. "Grandad does this a lot. We'll get him." I knew my cheeks were probably bright red. What would she think about our family now?

Horsefeathers! Thanks a heap, Grandad.

I knew everybody in my class probably thought I was in some kind of awful trouble. Stephen would probably whisper that I'd gone back to stealing again, something I hadn't done for five years, not since Dotty and I had our serious talk about Christ. But that wouldn't stop Stephen Dalton from spreading rumors. When all the time, *he* was the one who should have been called out of class. Grandad was more his relative than mine.

I took a shortcut through the fields to Horsefeathers. Having Grandad live with us, with his Alzheimer's getting worse and worse, just wasn't working out. Maybe the Daltons had the right idea. Maybe Grandad needed more care than Dotty could give him. Lots of old people live in nursing homes, and the Daltons could afford to put Grandad in a nice one. Something sure had to change. I could see myself being called to the principal's office every day for the rest of ninth grade.

~~~~~~~~~~~~~~~~~~~~~~~~~~~~

Orphan came running in from the pasture, bringing the sunshine with her. She'd been back at the pond with Moby and Cheyenne. She whinnied and came galloping. Clouds parted and moved on, as if driven away by Orphan's breeze.

She skidded to a stop in front of me on the other side of the paddock fence. Nickering her greeting, she tossed her head and nuzzled the top of my head over the fence. I reached up and gave her a quick hug. Then I dug into my backpack, fished out one of Jen's granola bars, and broke off half for Orphan.

"You better enjoy this, Girl," I said, scratching her jaw. "I had to fight off Stephen Dalton for it."

Remembering why I'd come, I yelled at the top of my lungs, "Grandad! Are you here?" This game of Hunt-the-Grandad was sure getting old fast. I wondered if Dotty had even thought twice about calling me out of school. I should have asked Ms. Whitmore for my assignment before I left. I wasn't about to call and ask Stephen for it. Four days of class and already I'd fallen behind.

I kissed Orphan and trotted to the barn for phase two of Hide 'n' Seek. I checked the Horse-feathers office, the loft, each stall. I even climbed to the barn roof and yelled for Grandad. At least the weather had turned nice. I didn't even need my jacket.

Sugar came nosing around when I climbed down from the roof, so I took time out to give her a granola bar. She gobbled it and begged for more. I wished I had more time to play with her.

But I had to keep looking for Grandad. I took a deep breath and prayed, *God, help me not to be so mad at Grandad. And show me where he is.*

I put the bitless hackamore on Orphan and jumped on bareback. Instead of combing the pastures, I got another idea. If I were Grandad, I reasoned, where would I go? I'd want to go somewhere good. I'd want to go home. Grandad didn't really have a home any longer. Dotty's and B.C.'s and my house was his home now, but that wasn't the same. He'd sold the farmhouse he'd lived in for 60 years.

The farmhouse. Maybe that's where he'd run off to. Maybe in his mind, his home was still there.

"Come on, Orphan," I whispered, urging her with the slightest squeeze of my thighs.

She responded by lurching into a gentle canter. We cantered down the lane and across the field until I saw Grandad's old farmhouse sitting by itself on a hill, almost hidden by trees. "Whoa," I said when we reached the front lawn.

I wasn't sure who had bought the house or why, but nobody had moved in yet. Grass had grown long and wild around the broken-down porch. The two-story home of Reba and Jared Coop looked as worn-out as my grandfather.

"Grandad!" I yelled.

Something under the porch scratched. Squirrels ... or rats. It made me shiver. The front window of the old wooden house was broken. I rode Orphan as close to the window as I could get and tried to peer in. There was no sign of Grandad.

I slid off Orphan and walked to the side window. I could see the sagging empty bedroom, the pale green paint peeling from the walls and wet wood floor rotting. We moved to the back of the house.

Suddenly the door to the cellar slammed open. My heart jumped, and so did Orphan. Grandad Coop came barreling up the cellar steps.

10

"Grandad!" I shouted from the top of the steps. I stared down into the dark cellar that looked like a black, bottomless pit. "Are you okay?"

"Air," he muttered, stopping on the step directly below me, as if he couldn't get any farther. "Need air."

"You need air?" I asked, not sure I'd heard him right.

Grandad held an empty jar in one hand and the gold metal lid in the other. It was the kind of container people like the Hat Lady used for homemade pickles or jellies. "Need air!" he shouted, so loud this time I heard him all right.

"It's a gorgeous day up here, Grandad. Come on up," I said stepping backwards out of his way. "Get some fresh air out here. It stinks down there."

Rotting, dead musty smells seeped up from the dank, dark cellar. I felt sorry for Grandad, seeing him standing there, his old man smell mixing with cellar rot. And I felt guilty for wanting to pass him off on Stephen and his family.

"See how beautiful it is out here, Grandad? Come out in the fresh air with Orphan and me," I coaxed. "Want me to take that jar for you?" I reached for it, but he jerked away and hugged the jar to his chest as if it were the most precious thing in the world.

"Fine," I said. "You keep your jar. But we need to go home, Grandad. Dotty will be worried. You can't keep doing this, wandering off and worrying us all the time."

Grandad looked at me, but his eyes were empty. I could see myself, my watery reflection in those flat gray eyes better than I could see my grandfather through them. He wasn't home. That's how B.C. said it when Grandad disappeared so far inside himself we couldn't see him in his own eyes.

The glassy gray of Grandad's eyes made me think of Sugar. Her old gray mare's eyes had been flat like his before I started playing with her.

I got an idea. It was an instant revelation, just like I'd gotten when Stephen had chewed his pencil in language arts. "Grandad, are you bored?" Who wouldn't be bored—spending all day in that little room of his or staring at stupid TV shows? He had to get as bored as a Dalton Stable horse. Of course he was bored!

"Grandad, do you want to play?"

He didn't answer, but I thought he wrinkled his forehead.

"Come on a ride with Orphan and me." I had no idea how long it had been since my grandad had even been on a horse. I remembered him sitting on a bucking Buckskin when I was younger than B.C. was now. He'd dug his heels into the bronco and waved one arm in the air. But I hadn't seen him on a horse in maybe five years or more.

Still, suddenly it felt important for me to get him to ride—as important as life and death. As important as air.

I took Grandad's arm and walked him up on his old porch. He didn't try to pull away. I left him there while I jumped down and led Orphan as close as she could get to the edge of the porch. "Go ahead, Grandad," I said. "Climb on Orphan."

He didn't budge, didn't even try.

"Please? You're bored, Grandad. I know it." He didn't have the teeth to chew on wood like Stephen and Sugar. But those silent dull eyes said it all. "How about a ride on Orphan? Just one little ride?"

I told Orphan to stay. Then I climbed back up on the porch and stood beside Grandad. "Watch, Grandad!" I slid onto Orphan's back from the porch. She didn't move an inch. "See how easy it is? Come on!"

I patted Orphan's broad back behind me and scooted as far forward on her withers as I could. I breathed a prayer to God. "Do just like I did, Grandad."

And without warning, he did. Without dropping jar or lid, Grandad slid onto Orphan behind me.

"Yes! You did it! Hold on, Grandad! Can I take your jar for you? I won't drop it."

He shook his head no. At least he'd heard me. He was responding. It was working—just like it was working with Sugar.

I moved Grandad's arms to either side of me and tried to get him to wrap them around me. His arms felt bone-stiff, but he was trying to hold on—as much as he could without letting go of his jar.

"Walk," I told Orphan. She seemed to understand the fragility of her cargo and stepped softly, easing each hoof solidly as we walked away from the house toward Horsefeathers.

Grandad made a squeaky noise, like a squeal.

I turned back to see him. "Are you okay?"

He was looking up into the sky, and the corners of his mouth turned up. "Air," he whispered.

The sun shone on us. The faint scent of

smoke wafted across the pasture, mixing with the fresh smell of grass, clover, and Orphan. "Fresh air, Grandad. Hold on!" I shouted, pulling his arms around my waist and placing one hand on his knobby knee. "Canter!"

Orphan eased into a canter that flowed as gently as her walk. Grandad laughed. I felt tears evaporate from my cheeks as we floated together through the pasture, my grandfather's arms locked around me in the closest thing to a hug I'd ever gotten from him.

I felt him move his arms away. "No, Grandad!" I yelled. "Hold on!"

"Air!" he said and laughed again. His knees pressed firmly into Orphan, and I was amazed at the strength I felt as I tightened my own grip on his leg.

Grandad held his arms straight out at his sides as if they were wings helping us fly. Then with the jar in his right hand and the lid in his left, he brought his hands together over his head and clapped lid and jar together. I looked up and saw him twist the lid onto his jar without any trouble at all.

He let out a loud laugh that turned into a wheeze he couldn't seem to stop. I brought Orphan down to a walk and turned her toward our house. "Are you okay, Grandad?" I asked, frightened by the rasping deep in his chest. But he didn't say anything.

Dotty almost fainted when we rode up. "Father in Heaven, thank You!" she shouted. "Scoop, what in tarnation are you up to?" But she was laughing and crying at the same time.

B.C. came running from the backyard. "Grandad's riding Orphan!" he said in a singsong voice. "Grandad's riding Orphan."

"Can you slide off first, Grandad?" I asked.

He didn't answer me. He clutched his jar to his chest and wheezed.

I threw my right leg over Orphan's neck and managed to jump down, but Grandad didn't seem to notice. I stared up at him, but his eyes were glazed over. A curtain had gone down again, separating Grandad from us and the rest of the world.

Dotty helped me pull Grandad off Orphan. He almost knocked both of us over when he finally came down. But the jar stayed tucked under his arm.

"Come on inside, Jared," Dotty said, leading him toward the house. "I got chocolate pudding. Would you like that?"

B.C. sat down on the edge of the porch. "I thought Grandad was *home*," B.C. said, dangling his bare feet over the edge and kicking the side of the porch.

"He *was* home, B.C.," I said. "While we rode Orphan through the pasture, I know he was. I wish you could have been there to see it."

I walked Orphan back to Horsefeathers, cooled her off and turned her out. Then I finished chores. I tossed the ball around with Sugar for a while and fed her in little portions again. But my heart wasn't in it.

Grandad *had* been *home*. I was sure of it. But it hadn't lasted. And I wondered if Grandad would ever really be home again.

F riday morning I woke up to the sounds of crying. At first I thought I'd imagined it. Sunlight was just starting to shine through my window.

I scooched up in bed and saw B.C. sitting in the corner of my room, his knees pulled up to his chest. He was sobbing.

"B.C.? What's wrong?" I got out of bed and shivered, padding in bare feet to the corner of my room, where the ceiling dipped so low I had to duck.

He shook his head and kept his face buried in his knees and cried louder.

I slid down beside him. "Tell me what's wrong, B.C.," I begged.

He seemed so small, curled up like that on the floor still in his flannel pajamas that were a size too small for him. For as long as I could remember, B.C. had had these crying jags. Sometimes they lasted for hours until none of us could stand it. I wondered if he'd cried like this before our parents were killed in the explosion at the bottle plant. I couldn't remember.

What I did remember was little B.C., barely 2 years old, waiting by the door night after night, even weeks after the funeral, as if our dad would walk in like regular and pull out a pocketful of bottle caps for his son.

"Why—why—can't I keep—happy?" B.C. got it out in between sobs, wiping his snotty nose with his pajama sleeve. "I hate feeling like this, Scoop. I don't like this part."

"I know, B.C." I thought about how I'd wished I could keep the good parts of everything too—seeing Sugar respond to me, riding Orphan, hearing that Jake thought I was cute— and dump the bad parts. "But remember what Dotty says—about us, about Grandad, about everything? It's all part of life's package. A package deal. The sad stuff and the happy stuff—it's all part of you, B.C. And you're great!"

He put his chin on his knees and rocked back and forth, sniff-gasping air in sporadic jerks, the end signs of all-out crying.

Dotty came and took over. B.C. was still crying softly when I left the house, but Dotty had gotten him dressed, fed, and washed up.

I had to hurry to get the chores done at Horsefeathers. Then halfway to school it hit me. It was Friday. The mixer was Friday night. Tonight. Flashes of excitement took turns with waves of panic and terror as I ran the rest of the way to school.

West Salem High School buzzed with talk of

the mixer. I couldn't help but pick up everybody else's enthusiasm. Four or five kids asked me if I was coming to the mixer, and it felt kind of good to say yes for a change.

At lunch Maggie 37 Yellow whisked me away to the girls' bathroom. She wore a yellow jumper and had her hair tied up in a ponytail with a yellow ribbon.

"Scoop," she said, pushing her way to the mirror and dragging me with her, "I can't wait for the mixer! Matthew wanted us to go together, but so did Jacob and that new boy, Ty Something. So I told all of them I had to get to the gym too early to set things up so I'd meet them there." Maggie skillfully untied her hair and made it part in the middle, changing her accent to Scottish.

"As for you, young lassie," she said, "I've got a wee bit of an idea for this fine head of hair."

Maggie went to work on my braid, undoing it and brushing it hard until I thought I'd scream. Then she French-braided a tiny strand on both sides of my head and brought them together in the back. I closed my eyes while she pinned and sprayed and yanked.

When I opened my eyes, I could hardly believe it.

"Wow!" said Amanda, a freshman who almost never speaks to me. "You look great, Scoop! Terrific hair!"

I felt the braids and stared at my reflection in the smudged bathroom mirror. I liked what I saw. "Thanks, Maggie," I said.

The bell rang. "Take good care of that hair for tonight!" Maggie yelled as girls clamored out of the bathroom. "I'll see you at the mixer!"

I was the last one out of the john and almost late to class. It may have been my imagination, but I think almost everybody in fifth period turned and did a double take when I walked in.

"I like your hair," whispered the girl next to me.

I smiled a thanks and felt my cheeks warm. Now all I had to worry about was something to wear.

~~~~~~~~~~~~~~~~~~~~~~~~~~~~~~~~

Before seventh period I spotted Jen Zucker down the hall. "Jen!" I shouted.

She squinted at me over the stack of books she was carrying. I ran up to her, and she nodded at my hair. "Maggie 37?" she asked.

"You guessed it," I answered.

"Looks nice," she said. "Hey, why don't you come over early before Jake and Ray come to pick us up?"

"I'll do chores and get there as soon as I can after supper," I said. "Thanks, Jen."

After school I headed straight for Horse-feathers, trying hard not to bend my head too much and wreck Maggie's hairstyle. I knew B.C. would have laughed at the way I kept my neck stiff even when I was climbing the fence. Or maybe B.C. wouldn't have laughed. I hoped he was over his crying fit by now.

A car was parked in front of the barn and it took me a minute before I recognized Mrs. Cravens behind the wheel. I started for her car when I heard Caroline shout from the barn: "Scoop! Come here! Quick!"

I ran to the barn, hoping nothing was wrong with Sugar. "What's the matter, Caroline? Is it Sugar?"

"Yes!" she squealed. "You fixed her, didn't you?" She ran back to Sugar's stall, with me on her heels.

The formerly "old gray mare" didn't look at all old. She was out in the paddock rolling in the dirt beside Orphan. Sugar rolled over, then scrambled to her feet and came trotting up to us when Orphan did.

"She even *looks* different!" Caroline said. "What did you do to her?"

I put my arm around Orphan's neck and pressed my face to her mane ... until I remembered my hair. Straightening myself and trying to smooth my hair, I said, "Caroline, I played with Sugar."

"You played with her?" she repeated.

I nodded.

Caroline shrugged. "So can I ride her now?" she asked.

I didn't have time for that, but it wouldn't have been a good idea even if I hadn't had a mixer to go to. "I'd rather keep playing with her for a while. You don't want your horse to think the only thing you want from your friendship is to ride her or show her, do you?"

Caroline shook her head slowly. Then she turned and stared up at me. "What do you mean?"

"I mean that horses are more than beasts we can show or jump or race. For some reason only God knows, He made these big, strong animals so they would like us and accept us as friends. Sugar can be your best friend if you'll let her."

Orphan nudged me, making both Caroline and me laugh. "Just ask Orphan if you don't believe me."

Caroline threw her arms around her horse. "I believe you, Scoop. You're even better with horses than Ray said!"

I ran back to the barn and pulled carrot crispies and granola bars from my pack. Then I gave them to Caroline with a beach ball. "Now you and Sugar play while Orphan and I do chores." I remembered that Mrs. Cravens was still sitting in her car. "Caroline, what about your mother?"

"Oh yeah," she said. "I forgot. She has

errands. I'll go tell her it's okay with you if I stay. It *is* okay, isn't it?"

"It's more than okay," I said.

I led Orphan in to brush her and heard Mrs. Cravens' car drive off. For the next half hour I kept Caroline playing with her horse while I mucked stalls and picked hooves and brushed horses—all the while trying to protect my hair.

When I finished chores, I helped Caroline brush Sugar down. I hoped Caroline's mom wouldn't be late. It was after 4:00, and I still had a lot of getting ready to do before the mixer.

We finished cleaning Sugar's hooves and led her to the pasture when a car turned into the lane. Relief rushed through me. As soon as Caroline left, I could get home and take my bath and start getting my clothes together for the mixer.

A horn honked.

"There's Mom!" Caroline shouted. Sugar flicked her ears. I led the mare in from the paddock.

Peering into the barn, I could just make out that Caroline and her mother weren't the only people there. Then Caroline emerged from the barn with her mom and dad on either side. And the last shadow to take form was Jake Cravens.

12

I stared stupidly as Jake passed his parents and sister and walked right up to Sugar and me. His teeth looked even whiter than before, and his smile showed every gleaming tooth.

"What are *you* doing here?" My voice asked the question before my mind could take hold of the words and stop them. How stupid! Why *wouldn't* he be here? These were his parents, his sister, their horse!

Jake's smile shrank as he reached up to scratch Sugar's ears. "We're on our way home," he said.

"I'm sorry," I stammered. "I didn't—"

"So! Let's see this amazing new horse Caroline claims she has!" Mr. Cravens wore a gray uniform and a cap that matched. It looked like the gas company uniform Mr. McCarthy wears to our house to read the meter.

"Daddy!" Caroline protested, tugging his hand and dragging him closer. "See for yourself! Doesn't Sugar look different?"

Caroline's mother eyed the mare, studying her from both sides. "Hope you don't mind the audience," she said. "I picked up the rest of the family on the way here. Is she really responding already? Have you gotten her to perform?"

"Looks like the same old gray mare we left here, if you ask me," said Mr. Cravens.

"I think she looks better," Jake said.

I didn't dare look at him. I wondered if my hair had stayed as nice as it had looked in the girls' bathroom.

"Who, son?" Mr. Cravens asked, chuckling. "Scoop or the horse?"

I hoped my face didn't turn as red hot as it felt. "Sugar's a good horse," I said, not knowing what else to say.

"Do you mind if we watch Caroline ride her?" asked Mrs. Cravens.

"Now?" I asked, adding up the minutes in my head, counting how much time I'd have to get ready for the mixer.

"Just a short ride?" said Mrs. Cravens.

"Could we, Scoop?" Caroline got in my face to ask, pleading with her little triangular eyes.

I sighed. "Sure," I said. Caroline cheered, and Sugar bobbed her head at the racket. I was pretty certain Sugar would be a better ride already, but I still wished I could have had a chance to ride her first.

Only Caroline followed Sugar and me into the cross-ties, where I saddled and bridled the mare and outfitted Caroline with a safety helmet. I was glad nobody else came with us. If Jake had followed us, I probably wouldn't have been able to do anything right.

"Now Caroline," I said, helping her mount her horse. Sugar held still, but she pawed the ground once after her rider was on her back. "The most important thing to remember is *have fun*. Got it? This is your buddy, and you're going out to have a great time with her. Nobody else exists but you and your horse."

Sugar followed me, her nose only inches from my back. I hoped she wouldn't slobber on my hair. We walked past the spectators. All three Cravens had bunched to the center of the paddock arena.

"Go Caroline!" Jake yelled. Then he flashed a grin to me that seemed to travel straight through me, warming even my fingertips.

I started to call out a trot, then stopped. The last thing I wanted Caroline or her horse to feel was that they were in some kind of a horse show. Caroline clicked in the back of her throat, and Sugar strode into a faster walk until it broke to a slow trot.

"Now that's good, right?" asked Mr. Cravens.

"Sugar has a nice, easy trot," I said.

Caroline bounced too much. She needed to use her legs more. But her smile told me how happy she felt to be on Sugar. The rest would come. They trotted all the way around the ring twice.

"Urge her on!" I called. "Use your legs! Squeeze with your knees."

Caroline must have done it because Sugar picked up the pace, trotting faster and faster until I was afraid Caroline might bounce completely out of her saddle. Then Sugar stretched into a gentle lope, a slow canter that took every bouncing movement away from her rider.

Mrs. Cravens let out a short gasp.

Thank You, God, I prayed.

"That's good, isn't it?" Mr. Cravens asked his wife.

"Yes, Honey," she answered. "That's *very* good. I believe we got the right horse after all— *and* the right trainer!"

Beside me I heard Jake whisper, "You did it, Scoop! You're amazing!"

I might have burst with pride right then and there if I hadn't had my new hairdo to protect. I turned back at Jake just in time to meet his grin.

I glanced at my watch: 4:42. If they didn't leave now, I'd never get ready in time to go to Jen's early. There was so much to do. Guys were lucky. I figured it would probably take Jake all of two minutes to get ready for the mixer. I wondered if during those two minutes, he might think about me.

"Isn't Sugar wonderful?" Caroline squealed. She stopped her horse and got off. "She didn't even want to stop! I had to pull her in!"

"It's a miracle," her dad conceded. "I guess we really do have a horse after all." Mr. Cravens stuck out his hand for me to shake. "Thanks, Scoop. We'd like you to board Sugar for a couple of months if that's all right with you."

"It sure is," I said. *Thank You, God*. Even Jen would have to admit Horsefeathers Stable was doing all right money-wise.

Mr. and Mrs. Cravens trailed off to the car. Caroline held the reins while I unsaddled Sugar.

As soon as I had the saddle in my arms, Jake whisked it to his. "I'll put this by the tack box for you," he said. Then more softly: "See you tonight, Scoop."

I watched him walk away and into the barn.

"Should we brush her now?" Caroline asked.

"Hmmm?" I asked, Jake's voice still echoing in my ear. "Oh that's okay, Caroline. I'll do it. Your parents are waiting for you. Maybe you could come back and ride again when Maggie's here to show you a couple of tricks. And when

Carla, our friend, gets back, you might want to sign up for lessons with her. How's that sound?"

"That sounds great!" Caroline said. She turned to me, a huge smile spread all over her face. "You're great too, Scoop! And I'm not the only one who thinks so!" She turned and trotted off to the car with her family.

Caroline's not the only one who thinks I'm great? Horsefeathers! Did she mean her brother thought so too?

Just as I finished turning out Sugar, thunder rumbled in the distance. I looked up to see gray clouds moving east across the darkening sky. I had to get home fast, before the rains came and ruined my hair.

Halfway home, the sky flashed and thunder rattled. The wind picked up. I ran with my arms over my hair. The sky grew darker. Just as I reached our front lawn, lightning split the sky. It looked like a white winter tree, barren branches stretching to heaven. I hopped up on the porch and tore through the front door, running smack into somebody.

"Mrs. Powers?" It felt funny to see the Hat Lady in our living room. If West Salem were an old English society, Mrs. Powers would have been the aristocracy and we would have been the peasants. She looked out of place in a small black hat that fit the top of her head like an English saddle. Then I remembered that Dotty said some of the church women were taking turns looking in on Grandad.

"Scoop!" she said in her breathless, high-pitched voice that trembled when she sang hymns in church. It trembled now. "Oh dear, I'm so glad you're home! I was just about to go look for him myself!"

"Grandad's missing again? Horsefeathers! Not again!" I said, my stomach tightening in knots. How could he be gone again? Why couldn't they just—

"I turned my back for 30 seconds and just like that, he was gone!" Mrs. Powers touched her hat, held it to her head as if she feared it might blow off. "It can't have been longer than five minutes. He couldn't have made it very far."

"Where's B.C.?" I asked, a hopeless feeling creeping into me.

She sighed and shook her head. "Your brother came home from school and went straight to Dotty's room. He won't come out, Dear. He's all right though. I hear him playing with those bottle caps of his."

Great. And no sign of Dotty. It was up to me.

I stormed out to the front porch. Lightning shot a jagged bolt that seemed aimed right at me. A crack of thunder followed on its heels. Cupping my hands to my mouth, I yelled into the wind, "Grandad! Where are you? Come inside!"

Grandad was probably trying to go back to his old farm again. I'd taken the shortcut home from Horsefeathers and hadn't passed him in the fields. Maybe he'd walked off down the lane toward the main road.

I jumped off the porch and raced to the lane, yelling for Grandad while the wind whipped my hair across my face and in my mouth. How much longer was this going to keep happening? It wasn't fair.

Lightning flashed and I caught a glimpse of a lone figure at the end of the lane. It looked like a scarecrow and had to be my grandfather. "Grandad!" I yelled, running to him. He didn't turn around, but kept shuffling in tiny steps down the lane.

He was staring up at the sky, and when I got close I saw he had the old mayonnaise jar in his hands. It stank like sour milk. "Come back home!" I shouted, grabbing his wrist and turning him around. His wrist was so skinny my fingers wrapped all the way around.

He tried to pull away, then gave in and let me tug him toward the house. A giant raindrop splatted on my forearm. I kept hold of Grandad with one hand and tried to protect my hair with the other. "Hurry, Grandad!"

More drops hit around me, on me. I jerked and pulled at Grandad to hurry him up, but he took his stiff, tiny baby steps. The sky opened and dumped water on us in hard sheets that soaked into my soul. I gave up trying to save my hair. Every inch of me was heavy with rain. I couldn't keep living like this. Something had to give, and I was sick and tired of having it be *me*.

13

At the front porch, Grandad kept his legs so stiff I almost had to lift him to get him up the steps and into the house. B.C. and the Hat Lady were standing in the doorway holding the door open.

"Jared, Jared, Jared!" cried Mrs. Powers. "Mercy, mercy! What are we going to do with you?"

I knew what *I'd* like to do with him. And I hoped God would forgive me for the thought. I took time out and asked Him to. B.C. stood back a few paces and stared at us. At least he had stopped crying.

"I'll take care of your grandpa, Scoop. You go on in and get out of those wet clothes, Darling." Mrs. Powers led Grandad off to his room.

I hurried to the bathroom to check the damage. The rain had mixed with Maggie's hairspray to form glue that made my hair hang in globs. It felt sticky and smelled weird.

Beauty is on the inside, not the outside, Dotty always said. Well she better be right—at least for tonight. With less than an hour to go before Ray and Jake picked us up, outside beauty sure wasn't one of my options.

I started the bathtub filling when the phone rang. I listened. Nobody answered it. The phone rang. And rang. And rang.

I threw open the bathroom door and stormed out to the living room. "Fine," I muttered. "*I'll* get it. Don't anybody bother themselves."

"Hello. What do you want?" I yelled into the phone.

There was a silence on the other end of the line.

"What?" I shouted. "Are you selling something? Because we're not buying. Got it?"

"Um ... Scoop? Is ... is that you?" It was a guy's voice. It was Jake's voice.

"Oh no! I ... Jake?" I managed to say, wanting to hang up, to shrivel up.

"Well ... Ray said to call. My uncle thought you might like us to pick you up at your house instead of Jen's, with the rain and all?" Jake sounded like he was afraid of me.

"That would be so nice," I said in as sweet a voice as I could muster.

"Okay then," Jake said, sounding anxious to get off the phone. "We'll see you in about a half hour." He hung up.

Horsefeathers! So much for pretty on the inside.

The bath water! I ran to the tub and shut it off just as it overflowed, dripping onto the floor.

It was the fastest bath and hair-washing on record. I had to towel dry as best I could. We had a hair dryer once, but it blew out and we never got another one. When I came out of the bathroom, Dotty was home.

"Scoop, I'm so sorry! Addy told me how you had to go out in the storm after your grandad." Dotty's hair stuck to the sides of her head. She was barefoot, and her grocery store uniform looked soaked. But I was feeling too sorry for myself to feel sorry for her. "Can I fetch you something to eat?"

"Jen and everybody are coming by to pick me up in 10 minutes, Dotty!"

Her eyebrows came together in a bushy "V" above her thick, brown glasses. She'd forgotten.

"The mixer?" I said, hearing the edge in my voice. "You knew I was going."

"At school! That's right. You ain't dressed, Scoop!" She pushed me toward the stairs, as if *she* had to convince *me* to hurry. "Go on! Git! I'll fetch your grandad a bite to eat."

I tore up the stairs, pulled off my jeans, looked in my closet for 10 seconds before settling on the turquoise sweater I'd worn to school Wednesday. My hair still felt wet, but I did the best I could brushing it down and to the side. I hoped Jake liked the wet look.

I was still fussing with my hair when a thought struck me the same instant thunder roared and shook my windowpane. What if Jake and Ray came inside? Or even to the front door?

I raced down the stairs to the living room. Grandad's wet clothes lay scattered about like manna in the wilderness. His overalls dangled over the back of his old rocking chair. A wet towel pile had sprouted in the middle of the floor.

I picked up stuff, throwing everything over one arm until I couldn't carry any more. With my foot, I scooted Grandad's rocker around so you couldn't see the strip of duct tape on the seat. I heard Dotty chattering to Grandad in the kitchen. I'd just throw everything in Grandad's room and let Dotty sort it out later.

Jake would be here any minute.

Grandad's door was cracked open enough for me to stick my foot in and open it the rest of the way. I heaved the pile of wet clothes and towels into his room. A stench so foul, so rotten came from his room it stopped me in my tracks. The smell was so strong I was afraid somebody in the living room or at the front door might be able to smell it.

I ventured into his room and got down on my knees to look under Grandad's bed. There was the mayonnaise jar, with molding mayonnaise still in the bottom of the glass. I reached under and pulled it out, almost gagging at the stink. Two smaller jars blended odors of rotten pickles and moldy mustard. I grabbed them too and headed to the kitchen to trash them.

Dotty, Grandad, and B.C. were eating sandwiches and potato chips. I scurried through and opened the cabinet under the sink to get to the trash can.

All of a sudden I was hit from behind. Something grabbed at my arm, and I felt sharp fingernails digging into my hand. "Air!" Grandad yelled, grabbing at the jars in my hand. "My air!"

"Stop it, Grandad!" I shouted. "You're hurting me!" He wanted the jars. But if I let go of them, they might break.

He shoved me with a force I didn't think he still owned. I stumbled, lost my balance. The jars crashed to the floor an instant before I did. My head bounced on linoleum and knives stabbed my hand.

"Help!" I screamed. My arm hurt. I'd landed on it crooked. A piercing pain ripped through my forearm and made me shut my eyes so tight tears squeezed out.

When I opened my eyes, I saw red. Blood. Blood on my arm. Blood on the floor. Blood on my turquoise sweater.

Dotty was on her knees beside me, kneeling on broken glass and saying something I couldn't understand. I couldn't understand it because someone was screaming. Loud and high and steady. B.C. stood a few feet away from me yelling at the top of his lungs.

It's okay, B.C.! I wanted to say. But I didn't feel okay.

"Scoop!" Dotty screamed right next to my ear. She took my hand and pain stabbed my forearm.

"Don't!" I cried, pulling my hand down and hurting my arm again.

"The blood ain't from your arm, Honey. Jesus, help me stop this girl's bleeding. It's your finger's been cut. You cut it real good. Help us, Lord."

She left my arm down and dabbed with the dishtowel at my bloody finger. I had to look away. I was afraid I was going to throw up.

"I'm wrapping this here towel tight so's it can't bleed no more. Thank You, good Lord, for being right here with us through this. Help B.C. to stop screaming." She wrapped the whole towel around my little finger, a boxer's glove on a toothpick.

"B.C., Honey," Dotty said. "I need you to stop screaming now."

He actually did. His mouth stayed open in a silent scream as he stared at me, at the blood.

"Can you sit up, Scoop? Lord, help Scoop sit up." Dotty helped me too. The room swirled, and I felt sick again and my arm killed me.

"We're going to the hospital!" Dotty announced. "B.C., you get your grandad. Come on, Hon."

"Ow!" I cried, struggling to my feet, with Dotty's chubby arms around my waist. "I can't go, Dotty." Tears poured down my cheeks. "Ray and Jen and Jake are coming for me. The mixer."

"They'll understand. You ain't going nowhere but the hospital."

I knew she was right. But I almost couldn't stand it. I let her put her coat over my shoulders and help me outside. Grandad and B.C. followed silently behind us. The rain came down steady and cold. It didn't matter that rain drenched my hair, not any longer.

It hurt to get into the car. It hurt when Dotty fastened my seat belt. It hurt when B.C. slammed the back door and Dotty shut Grandad's door.

Dotty started the engine and backed halfway down the drive before she remembered to put her lights on. "You're the light of the world, Jesus," she said as she pulled the knob. "Help us get there safe."

We had just turned onto the gravel road when I recognized the Cravens' station wagon coming from the other direction. "I don't want to see them!" I yelled, trying to stop crying. I didn't want *them* to see *me*.

Dotty stopped her car, and Ray's uncle

pulled up next to us. "Everything okay?" he asked.

"Well, not rightly," Dotty said, struggling to roll her window down.

"Is Scoop in there?" Ray yelled from the back seat. "Where are you going?"

"Scoop ... had an accident ... in the kitchen. We gotta go see to her at the emergency," Dotty said.

Rain beat on our car roof. I looked the other way, out my window that was streaked with rain-tears.

I heard Jen's voice: "Is Scoop okay? What happened? Did she burn herself?"

"Don't you worry none, Hon," Dotty said. "I think Scoop may need stitching in her finger. And she may have done broke her arm."

Somebody groaned. Somebody said, "Oh no."

"Do you need any help?" It sounded like Jake asking.

"No. You go on. You can tell Scoop all about that mix thing tomorrow. We got to git." Dotty hit the gas so hard the car screeched and jerked ahead.

I peeked over my shoulder as their station wagon disappeared. Through the window I could see Jake and an empty seat next to him that would have been—should have been—mine.

14

The rest of the night blended into one long, horrible nightmare. At the hospital we had to sit in the waiting room with a man and woman who screamed at each other and smelled like whiskey. I stared down at the speckled gray linoleum tiles until my head felt like I was under water. When I looked up, white ceiling tiles and pale green walls stared back.

A guy who'd been shot was wheeled past us on a stretcher. The way he thrashed from side to side, forcing three ER guys to hold him down, made me think he could be okay. Dotty took it all in and asked the reception lady and nurses details on everybody who came through.

"That poor boy!" Dotty exclaimed as they wheeled the shooting victim through double silver doors. "Where's his mama?" She stood on tiptoes to peer through the round glass windows down the hallway where he'd disappeared.

When the nurse finally got to me, I almost felt guilty for taking up space in the emergency room since I hadn't been in a brawl or a shootout. The doctor put 12 stitches in my finger and said it was good Dotty stopped the bleeding, but next time we might not want to use the soiled dish towel.

The X-rays of my arm killed me. They twisted my bones in ways bones shouldn't ever go. Each time after making me stretch my arm in a new way, the X-ray doctor stepped out of the dark room and left me on the examining table by myself. With herself safely out of the dark room, she shot invisible rays into my arm. When she informed me that we had to do some of the X-rays over, I started crying like a baby.

I had to move to a different cubicle for someone to check my heart and shine a tiny flashlight in each of my eyes. Finally, the main doctor reappeared and called Dotty into my little cubicle. He had thick black hair that looked hard to comb. His English was a lot better than ours, but he looked like at least one of his parents may have come from India or another country.

"Is she going to be okay, Doc?" Dotty asked. She held both her hands up to her heart, as if she had to be prepared to stop her own heart attack if the doc came out with the wrong answer.

The doctor smiled at Dotty, showing slightly yellowed teeth. "She will be fine certainly," he said, pronouncing each consonant in a way that would make *certainly* easy to spell. "Your daughter has a tiny fracture."

Neither one of us corrected him on *daughter*.

"It's like a crack in one of the bones in her forearm close to the wrist. It should heal fast at her age." He turned to me. "I'd like you to wear this bandage and come back in a week—sooner if you experience any problems. Keep your arm in the sling so you don't do further injury. Do you understand?"

I nodded. Dotty thanked him a hundred thousand times.

"Can I go now?" I asked.

"Thank You, Lord," Dotty said, as I scooted off the examination table. "And thank You it's her left arm too."

I didn't echo with an Amen.

The doctor flung back the curtain, which was like a pale green cloth shower curtain, and Dotty led the way back to the emergency waiting room.

"There now! See?" said a heavyset nurse who reminded me of Dotty. Her pants and shirt looked like a white version of Dotty's black and orange Hy-Klas uniform. She hovered over Grandad and B.C., fussing with Grandad's collar. "Didn't I tell you the doctors would take real good care of her?"

Her words came out more like singing than talking. She gave me a headache. "And now you can all go home and get some sleep!" She twittered over to me and I flinched. "Are we feeling better, Honey?" she asked me.

I nodded yes for B.C.'s sake more than for the nurse's. B.C. stood up and took Grandad by the hand. They followed us out to the car through a cold drizzle that stuck to me like plastic wrap.

Nobody but Dotty talked on the drive home. Once again, she launched into her mission of talking to Grandad about Jesus and trusting Christ to forgive sin and give us eternal life. "We can't none of us earn heaven, Jared," she said earnestly. "It's a gift. Ain't nothing left up to us but to accept it and even that's through the Holy Spirit workin' in us."

Grandad didn't make a sound in return— not a throat-clear, not a harumph, not a cough. He might as well have been asleep.

As soon as Dotty shut off the engine, I slid out of the car and walked straight in the house and up to bed. My head hurt. My arm hurt. My finger throbbed. I fell into bed without changing out of my bloody turquoise sweater.

Minutes later I heard Dotty's plodding footsteps on the stairs. I knew she was coming to check on me, but I pretended I was already asleep.

Dotty sniffed from the doorway. With my back to her and my eyes shut tight, I heard her whisper, "Thank You for taking good care of Scoop, Lord. Poor little thing. If I could understand what You have in mind all the time, I guess You wouldn't be God." She sighed so deeply I thought I felt it. "Package deal. Right, Lord? Package deal."

~~~~~~~~~~~~~~~~~~~~~~~~~~~~~~~

Saturday I woke up with the sun but kept making myself go back to sleep. I couldn't face the pain. Pain in my finger. Pain in my arm. Pain in my heart when I thought about everybody else at the mixer.

I didn't want to see anybody—except Orphan. I missed my horse. It felt like 24 years since I'd been with her instead of 24 hours.

Dotty came in about mid-morning to tell me Jen called. She and Maggie and Ray were handling chores. I wasn't to worry. And she didn't have to go into Hy-Klas until second shift.

I went back to sleep, drifting in and out of crazy dreams filled with runaway horses and mountains of bottle caps and glass jars. Every dream ended with me falling from something. I'd jerk myself awake, the bed still shaking from my dream fall.

Three or four times I opened my eyes to find B.C. standing over me or lurking in the doorway staring in. I shut my eyes and rolled over, not even wanting to see my brother. I'd planned to spend all weekend playing with Sugar and riding her for Caroline. Now I couldn't do anything.

And I didn't even care.

It was dark again when Dotty made me get up and come downstairs. I still had on my bloody sweater. My jeans smelled like the hospital waiting room. My lips were cracked, and my tongue felt hairy.

At the table with Dotty and B.C., I picked at the lukewarm spaghetti oozing its watery orange sauce onto the yellowed plastic plate in front of me.

"Phone's been ringing off the hook all day for you," Dotty said. "You got nice friends, Scoop. Thank You, Lord, for good friends."

"Ray called and I talked to him," B.C. said.

"You didn't tell him anything, did you?" I asked, imagining B.C. replaying the whole ugly story.

B.C. shook his head. "I just said you were sleeping." He looked better. The black circles under his eyes had melted into tiny, gray lines. I felt a little better too, although I wasn't about to admit it.

When I swallowed I felt the long, cold spaghetti strands slither down my insides like skinny worms. "I'm not hungry, Dotty," I said.

"Neither is Grandad," B.C. said. "Dotty says he's sick. I can't go in his room."

"Why would you want to?" I said too quickly, before I had a chance to stop myself. I glanced at Dotty, then at my plate. "Sorry," I muttered.

Dotty scooped another glob of potato salad on her plate. The yellow potato salad juice flowed into the watery orange puddle on her plate. "I was afeared Jared was poorly. Doc Lyle stopped by. He ain't sure but what your grandad's had hisself another little stroke. We'll get him into the office next week. But Doc says he's best to rest here for now. We can keep him just fine right here."

I wondered. Maybe the Daltons had been right all along. If they'd had their way and put Grandad in the nursing home, none of this would have happened. I would have gone to the mixer with Jake. And I'd be riding Sugar right now, instead of sitting around the house with my arm in a sling.

"I'm taking a bath and going back to bed, Dotty," I said, scooting away from the table.

That night it took me a long time to fall asleep. I closed my eyes and imagined what my life could have been like without all the bad stuff, what Grandad might have been like without Alzheimer's, what B.C. would have been like without his manic depression.

I knew Dotty would call everything part of the *package deal*. But the way I felt, as I lay in bed, my arm aching and my finger throbbing, I wanted to ask for a different package.

15

R ise and shine! Time to get ready to go to the Lord's house, Scoop. Don't want to keep the good Lord waiting!" The Sunday morning sun barely peeked into my bedroom, and Dotty sounded way too cheerful.

I rolled over in bed and pulled the covers over my head. My shoulder felt stiff, and my neck had a crick in it. "I can't go to church," I mumbled.

"Nonsense!" Dotty said, pulling back the covers. "It'll cure what ails you."

I rolled onto my back and squinted up at her. She was dressed in her navy-and-white polka-dot dress that fit too tight everywhere.

"Breakfast in five minutes, Scoop," Dotty said. She padded out of my room and down the stairs.

I groaned as I pulled myself up in bed and swung my feet around to touch the cold, wood floor. A shiver ran through me that made my finger start throbbing. I wondered if I could ever talk Dotty out of making me go to church. I did ache, but the real reason I didn't want to go was that I didn't feel like talking to anybody about the mixer I'd missed, or the "accident" I hadn't.

On my way downstairs I rehearsed the argument I'd try on Dotty. *Dotty, my arm is killing me. Boy, I wish I could go to church, but I can't. I promise I'll read the Bible on my own and watch TV church.*

Determined, I rounded the living room and strode to the kitchen. "Dotty, my arm—"

But the sight of Grandad sitting at the kitchen table stopped me cold. His back was to me. His bald head, spotted with tiny tufts of gray, stuck out of his flannel bathrobe. Scenes from Friday night rushed back at me like lightning flashes. I felt his powerful shove at the sink, heard him yelling for air. The jars slipped through my fingers again. I was falling, trying to catch myself but not being able to stop my body until my head bumped the linoleum and the light flashed in my brain, electrifying my arm and my finger.

"I'll take my bath first," I called in to Dotty.

The warm water felt good, melting and loosening my stiff muscles. I tried to keep the bandage dry by holding my arm over the side of the tub. Already my arm itched beneath the tan bandages.

"Move along now!" Dotty yelled through the bathroom door. "B.C.'s got to brush his teeth."

Grandad was back in bed by the time I came out to the kitchen. B.C. rushed past me to claim the bathroom. He wore his green suit that had to be a size too small for him, a white shirt and his Sunday shoes. Dotty had greased down his hair and combed it to part in the middle. He looked pretty normal though.

"Hi, Scoop," he said, turning back and wrinkling his whole face to look me over up and down. "Are you okay?"

"I'm okay, B.C.," I answered.

I sat down to cold fried eggs. "Dotty," I said, picking at the slippery white egg on my plate, "I don't think I'm ready to go out yet. Maybe I should stay home from church."

I expected her to jump right on me and tell me how important church was. Instead she didn't say anything for a minute. Then she lowered herself into the chair across from me at the table. She spooned four teaspoons of sugar into her white, cracked coffee cup.

"You know I'm a firm believer in church, Scoop," Dotty said. She took a sip of the coffee, then put in two more spoonfuls of sugar. "But the good Lord ain't bound by four walls an' a steeple. I reckon He can meet you here if you can't make it to His house this morning." Dotty dunked a powdered doughnut into her coffee cup and bit off half of the soggy doughnut, leaving a powder mustache on her upper lip.

I couldn't believe it. I'd been all set to do serious battle, and Dotty had given in at round one.

"Besides," she went on, "I ain't none too sure about your grandaddy this morning. He ain't up to going to church neither. I reckon one of us had oughta stick by home with him."

That changed things. No way was I staying alone in the house with him—not after what he'd done to me. What if he took it into his head to leave again? I wasn't going to stop him.

"On second thought, Dotty," I said. "Maybe you're right. Maybe I need to get out and go to church. I'm feeling better."

Dotty raised her bushy eyebrows at me. "Well, thank You, Jesus!" she said. "See how fast the good Lord answers prayer, Scoop? I reckon I can keep care of your grandad if you feel up to walking on with B.C. after you had some breakfast."

On the edge of the kitchen table lay Dotty's Bible, the corners worn and frayed—not from abuse, but from use. Dotty reached over and patted its bumpy, black cover. "I'll read to Jared from the Good Book."

Although I had to admit my arm felt better, it was tough getting dressed for church. I wanted to brush my hair into a ponytail, but I couldn't do it with one hand. Finally I let my hair hang where it wanted, and I walked downstairs for B.C.

Dotty was already in Grandad's room reading to him from the Gospel of John. B.C. was waiting for me on the front porch.

"We're leaving now, Dotty," I called in. "We've still got time to stop by Horsefeathers." I missed Orphan like crazy. Jen and Maggie said they'd do chores Sunday too, but I needed to see my horse.

B.C. overheard. "Cool! Can I feed them? I'll do the chores."

"You see you don't get your suit or shoes dirty, hear B.C.?" Dotty shouted. "Say a prayer for me and your grandad," Dotty called out. "We'll do the same for you."

Orphan was waiting for me when we reached the lane.

"Hey, Girl," I crooned, rubbing my face against hers and stroking her with one arm. I felt better, more like me, than I had for days. Horsefeathers is where I belong.

Nobody said I couldn't ride with my sling on. If we hadn't been on our way to church, I couldn't have stopped myself from climbing up and letting Orphan take me away from everything crummy.

Orphan sniffed my sling and arched her neck.

"Don't worry, ol' Girl," I told her. "I'm going to be okay."

"Want me to clean out the stalls?" B.C.

asked. He had the pitchfork in his hands and held it like a sergeant at arms.

"Not now, B.C.," I said, kissing Orphan good-bye. "Maybe later. Thanks."

We checked on Sugar before we left. She was grazing peacefully in the back pasture with Cheyenne. At least that seemed to be working out. The blue sky was already clouding up again. It didn't smell like rain yet, but I saw rain in the gray of the clouds.

B.C. and I cut across the field. We had to hurry to make it. From the sidewalk out front of the church, I heard organ music start up. People moved in noisy groups up the church steps and into the building. I stared at the ground and tried to be invisible.

"Scoop! I didn't think you'd come." Jen Zucker waved from the top step and met me halfway. "Are you okay? You look awful. What did you do to your arm? I thought it was your finger. Ray said you had stitches in your finger."

It was too many questions coming at me at one time. I guess I should have been glad that Maggie 37 was going to a different church now. She would have had 37 times as many questions as Jen.

"I cracked a bone in my arm," I said. "But it's okay. I can still ride."

Tommy Zucker pushed his way through the

crowd and stood between Jen and me. "Scoop, where did they sew you up? Can I see? Can I?"

"Tommy!" Jen scolded. "Go sit with Mom."

Travis came up. "Scoop," he said, touching my sling lightly. "Man, sorry to hear about your accident. What did you do, get hit by a frying pan?"

Then Mr. and Mrs. Zucker and four or five little Zuckers ran up and circled me, fussing until the choir started and we all had to sit down.

On the way to our pew, half a dozen people asked us where Dotty was, how Grandad was doing, what I'd done to my arm. I was relieved to get to our pew and away from the questions. The Hat Lady turned and winked at me in a way that made me think she knew what had really happened. I couldn't look at her. I wanted out of there.

B.C. scooted close to me without even begging to sit by Tommy.

Someone slid into the pew behind us and leaned forward, close to my ear. "Nice bracelet." Out of the corner of my eye, I glimpsed Stephen Dalton's red hair. That's all I needed to make my day complete!

I pretended I didn't hear him.

He whispered loudly, "I'll bet it's the nag we sent over from Dalton Stables, right? Did that old gray mare do that to you?"

"No!" I whispered without turning around.

"For your information, Sugar is doing just fine, thank you." Sugar was just about the only thing left in my life that *was* doing fine.

"Sure she is," Stephen whispered. "You just don't want to admit that you couldn't fix that horse. I can see why you wouldn't want everybody to know that an old mare got the best of the young horse whisperer."

"You don't know what you're talking about!" I whispered, turning to face off against his pea green eyes. "The old gray mare, as you call her, didn't do this. The old gray grandad did it!"

It just came out. I hadn't planned on saying it. But I wasn't sorry. Stephen should know— the Daltons should know—the truth. It wasn't fair for us to have to keep taking care of him by ourselves. They deserved to know.

"Oh fine," Stephen said, chuckling with disbelief. "Blame poor old Grandfather. My grandfather couldn't do that. He's too old and feeble. He hasn't even gotten out of bed since you've had him."

"You don't know anything, Stephen! He's gotten out of bed plenty! And who do you think has to go find him? Not you! Me!"

"Big deal," Stephen said. "I still think you got that arm falling off a horse. Grandad couldn't break your arm if he tried."

"You don't have any idea about him!" I said through clenched teeth. "He did this to me. This is his fault. And it's your fault too." I turned all the way around to face him. "You and your parents are the ones who should be taking care of him—not us."

Stephen twisted his lips to the side and winked at me. "Okay, Sarah Coop. No sweat. This is what we've been waiting for."

Suddenly my stomach felt sick. I couldn't remember what I'd just said. Why was I talking to Stephen Dalton anyhow? Of all people, why was I telling *him* the truth?

Stephen winked at me again as if we were conspirators, partners in a secret mission. "I'll take care of it. And I won't even tell where I got the information. Don't worry. I'll take care of everything."

I swung back around in my pew. B.C. had the hymnal open to the right page and he shoved it in my face. I mouthed the words as we sang through four verses, but my mind wasn't there. Stephen Dalton's words echoed in my ears: *I'll take care of everything.*

16

I wanted to get out of church as fast as I could, but people kept stopping me to ask about Dotty and Grandad and my arm. Jen followed me outside and down the church steps.

"Don't feel too bad about Friday night," she said. "You didn't miss all that much."

I looked up at her, trying not to be glad I didn't miss much. "Why?" I asked.

"Well, Ray talked about Carla the whole night. He must have asked me a dozen times when I thought she'd be back. And then Jake—"

Jen stopped to holler at the twins to quit hitting each other. She turned back to me, brushing something off her light blue dress. "What was I saying?" she asked.

"You said something about Jake," I urged.

"Oh yes. Jake didn't say much of anything. He's not much of a talker, Scoop. And he kept yawning all night. If you ask me, the whole mixer was boring."

It made me feel better even though I knew it shouldn't.

"So how *did* you hurt your arm?" Jen asked, keeping one eye on the twins. "Dotty didn't really say—just that you had a kitchen accident. I thought you'd burned yourself until Ray said you got stitches in your finger."

"I fell in the kitchen and twisted my arm and cut my finger," I said. It's what I should have said to Stephen. I wasn't sure myself why I'd told my worst enemy more than I'd told my best friend.

B.C. and I walked home, turning down several offers of rides. The sun that had forced its way through the clouds on our walk to church now hid behind grayer, fast-moving cloud swirls. I hoped it wasn't going to rain again.

We stopped by Horsefeathers and said hi to the horses again. *That Scoop is pretty cute.* I tried to hear the echo of Jake's words, but I couldn't. They were gone.

Finally B.C. and I headed home.

"Scoop," B.C. said when we were halfway home, "there's something I wonder about."

"Yeah, B.C.?" I said. "What?"

"Do you think it's my fault?" he asked.

"What, B.C.? Do I think what's your fault?"

"That Grandad's sick and that you hurt your arm?" His voice was soft as a horse's muzzle.

I stopped walking and stared at my brother. His hair had come un-slicked and his collar unbuttoned. He looked so sweet I wanted to cry.

"Your fault, B.C.? How could you think this was your fault?"

"Because I wanted my bedroom back. And I was mad at Grandad for hurting you."

"But you didn't do anything, B.C.," I said. "It's not your fault."

He shrugged and looked away. "It just feels like my fault sometimes," he said. "Everything does."

"B.C., that's not the way life works. I don't get a lot of the way it does work. But sometimes bad stuff just happens."

I reached out to hug him and forgot I still had one arm in a sling. "Ow!" I cried. "Now *that* was your fault," I said, making myself laugh so he would.

B.C. got it. He grinned. "Was not," he said.

We walked on in silence. I wondered what other thoughts floated around in B.C.'s head and never made their way out through his lips.

~~~~~~~~~~~~~~~~~~~~~~~~~~~~~~~

B.C. and I came in through the kitchen and found Dotty sitting by herself at the table, her Bible open in front of her.

"How's Grandad?" B.C. asked.

Dotty jumped as if she hadn't heard us come in. "Don't sneak up on a body like that, B.C.!" she said. She scruffed the top of his head. "Your grandaddy is doing poorly, Hon. I called the

134

doc. His Missus says she'll send him down to check in on Jared just as soon as he gets back from Warfield later tonight."

Dotty looked exhausted. The pink lipstick she'd put on for church had smeared her upper lip, and she hadn't finished combing her hair. Straightening herself and tugging at the hem of her polka-dot dress, she asked, "So how was church? Come sit a spell and tell me all about it."

B.C. managed to tell Dotty a lot more about the sermon than I'd gotten out of it. One glance around the kitchen told me Dotty had forgotten about dinner. While my brother rattled off the hymns we'd sung in church and Dotty exclaimed each song was her favorite, I scrounged the fridge to come up with something to eat. I came out with chicken noodle soup, Spaghetti-Os, and celery.

We were halfway through our meal and B.C.'s account of his plans to make a doghouse out of bottle caps for Dogless, the barn cat, when the phone rang.

"I'll get it," Dotty said, her chair legs groaning as they scraped the floor to let her push away from the table. The phone rang three more times before she crossed the living room and picked up the receiver.

"Hello?" Dotty's telephone voice always sounds like she expects the Prize Patrol to be on the other end, just waiting to drop a million dollars on her doorstep.

B.C. and I stopped eating. I tried to figure out who it was.

"Well, my, how are—" Dotty said, stopping as if somebody on the other end of the line interrupted her.

"Well, of course you can, but—" Whoever it was, wasn't letting Dotty get a word in edgewise.

"Now, now, Patricia, where'd you hear a thing like—"

"Who's Patricia?" B.C. asked.

"Shh," I said, trying to hear Dotty. Patricia had to be Patricia Dalton, Stephen's mother. I felt sick inside. Stephen must have told her what I'd said in church. My face burned as I held my breath and strained to hear Dotty's end of the conversation.

"Jared? No! That ain't a good idea. Kennsington? But—" Dotty sounded so upset, I could feel B.C. tense up. He started tapping his spoon on the table: *bang, bang, bang, bang.*

"I reckon we'll be here, but—" Dotty was cut off again. Then she hung the phone up gently. It was a minute before she walked back into the kitchen. When she did, she walked past us and stared out the screen door.

"What?" B.C. demanded, his banging spoon beating faster and faster. "Who was it?

What's wrong?"

"It's the Daltons," Dotty said, without turning around. "They're coming to pick up Grandad."

"No!" B.C. screamed. "They can't do that!" He tipped over his bowl of soup. His stool fell over when he jumped off and ran to Dotty's room. I heard the door slam.

Dotty didn't run after him like she usually did when he got upset. Instead, she kept staring out the kitchen door. "I can't figure it, Scoop," she said. "I knowed them Daltons wanted Jared in that fancy home for old folks. But they ain't never forced it like this here."

"What? What did they say, Dotty?" I asked, scared of what they might have said about me, about what I told Stephen. Stephen had said he'd take care of everything. This had to be what he meant.

"Hmmm?" Dotty said, as if she'd forgotten I was still there. "They said they knew he was poorly. But what I can't figure is why all of a sudden it's so all-fired important. They ain't even been over to see Jared in more than two weeks."

"When are they coming, Dotty?" I asked, wiping up B.C.'s mess.

"First thing this evening. 7:00. But I still can't figure it. Patricia seems dead set against

137

leaving her pa here. Lord, why does she have to go and yank her daddy out of his home now?"

She was asking God, but I knew why. Because of what Stephen must have told her. Because of what I'd told him.

But so what? It was all true. Grandad *did* run off. And he *did* make me break my arm. So maybe they were right. Maybe the Daltons had been right all along. Maybe Grandad didn't belong with us anymore.

I cleared the table by myself.

"We'll just have to change their minds when they get here. That's all there is to it," Dotty said, finally turning from the screen door. "Just don't let on about your accident, okay, Scoop? We ain't gonna lie, but there's no sense adding fuel to flames."

B.C. stayed in Dotty's bedroom the rest of the afternoon. Dotty sat by Grandad's bed and read her Bible. I wanted to go back to Horse-feathers, but I felt so tired all I could do was go to bed. I was too tired not to go to bed, but not tired enough to go to sleep. I tossed and turned while the shadows crept across my bedroom wall, and we all waited for the Daltons.

17

When I finally came downstairs Sunday evening, it was almost as dark inside as outside. I clicked on a lamp in the living room and heard Dotty talking to Grandad and Jesus in Grandad's room.

"Jared, I don't rightly know if you understand what I'm saying to you. I'm powerful sorry I didn't talk more about Jesus when you could hear me. Lord, I know You love this here soul more than I do. So I ain't worried. You'll do what's right by him. I'd just be mighty grateful if You could see fit to let me know he's headed home to You."

Grandad headed home? Dotty meant to heaven. I knew that. I'd known Grandad was sick, but not that sick. Was Dotty just saying all this because Grandad was leaving our house, or because he was leaving period?

My throat turned dry as sandpaper, and it hurt to swallow as I eavesdropped outside Grandad's room. What if the old man really was dying? And I was as much as sending him away myself.

I heard a car door slam outside. Then the sound of sharp, hushed voices grew louder. Footsteps marched up on the porch. Somebody knocked. "Dotty?" It was Patricia Coop Dalton.

I moved away from Grandad's door just as Dotty shuffled out of his bedroom. "I'll get it, Scoop," she said, sounding weary.

Ralph and Patricia Dalton stepped cautiously into our living room, as if they were afraid they'd catch some disease from breathing our air. They had on their church clothes, but then they almost always did. Ralph Dalton wore a navy business suit, and his wife had on a gray one. Both suits looked completely wrinkle free, and I wondered what they did—or didn't do— to keep their clothes like that.

Stephen trailed in after his parents and moved to the stairway, where he plopped down on the third stair. I glanced at him, and he gave me a secret wink, as if we were conspirators sharing a huge and dangerous secret. I looked away.

"Dotty," said Ralph, nodding his head at her by way of greeting, probably so he wouldn't have to touch her to shake her hand. "Is Jared ready to go? We're running a little late." He glanced at his watch to prove it.

"He ain't ready," Dotty said. "I made coffee."

"Dotty," he said, as if he were talking to a little child with half a brain, "now you know this is for the best. We can't have Jared running off

140

and getting hurt or staying here and hurting somebody." He glanced at me.

Dotty glanced at me too and tightened her lips. "Jared ain't never hurt nobody on purpose," she said. "He's doing just fine here. This is his home now. He's happy here with us."

"Ralph, I'm going to look in on Dad," said Stephen's mother. She and her husband moved to the doorway of Grandad's room and stared in. They looked like scared divers pausing for a deep breath before plunging into the bottomless sea. Then they plunged—in perfect step, left, right, in.

Dotty paced back and forth in front of me, her hands on her hips. She looked like a tea kettle ready to boil over. "I'd like to know how they found out about Grandad wandering. And you, Scoop!"

I couldn't answer. I hung my head.

She kept pacing. "Wouldn't you like to know who told them folks it was Grandad what pushed you?"

I glanced up at her. Dotty didn't even suspect that I was the traitor.

"Do you reckon it was them doctors at the emergency?" she asked. "Don't them nurses have to take some oath not to tell, like a *hypocrite* doctor-client oath? I'll tell you one thing. Doc Lyle wouldn't never have told, no sir."

Stephen was standing at my elbow. He leaned

into me and whispered, "See? Told you I'd take care of everything and keep you out of it."

"Lord Almighty," Dotty was praying, still pacing, "You changed Pharaoh's hard heart. Change these here Daltons."

Stephen's mother stepped out of the bedroom. "He looks just awful, Dotty," she said. Her eyes looked watery. "I don't think he knows me."

"Then you had oughta leave him be. He needs his sleep," Dotty said. "He don't need to be thrown out into that cold and plunked down in some nursing home."

Stephen's dad followed his wife into the living room. "Now, Dotty," he said. "I got Jared to wake up. I explained to him that we're taking him to a nice home with lots of people his own age and doctors and nurses who can take better care of him than you can here."

"You shouldn't oughta done that," Dotty said. "He'll fret now."

"No, I think he understood me, Dotty. He's putting his pants on right now."

"Perhaps we should discuss a few things, Dotty," Patricia Dalton said. "I don't want there to be any misunderstandings or hard feelings. We appreciate what you've tried to do for my father. But it just hasn't worked out."

Dotty stormed to the kitchen and began setting out cups and saucers. I moved to the arched entry between the living room and kitchen. I watched Dotty open cupboards and close them without getting anything out. She pulled a carton of milk out of the fridge and forgot to close the door. The refrigerator light spilled out on the dirty linoleum.

All the while, Patricia Dalton kept talking, following Dotty into the kitchen. "I know you mean well, Dotty," she said. "But he's *my* father, and I know what's best for him."

I heard the silverware drawer slam hard enough to rattle the knives, forks, and spoons. *Help Dotty*, I prayed. *And Grandad. And me.*

"You owe me big time!" Stephen whispered, standing so close behind me I could smell stale chocolate on his breath. His dad had pushed by me to sit at the kitchen table, leaving Stephen and me alone on the outskirts of the drama. B.C. still hadn't come out of Dotty's room.

I didn't answer Stephen. My stomach ached with guilt. Grandad was leaving on account of me, on account of what I said to Stephen in church. I didn't plan it, but it was what I had wanted. I didn't want to have to be called out of school to hunt for him. I didn't want to have him push me again, break my other arm. So why did I feel like a big hole inside me was growing bigger, swallowing up something I needed to survive?

I leaned against the wall just inside the kitchen to steady myself.

"I ain't giving Jared up without a fight!" Dotty declared. I had never heard my aunt so fierce in the seven years we'd lived together.

"He's *my* father!" exclaimed Patricia Dalton, sounding about two years old. "He'll get round-the-clock care in Kennsington."

"Bosh!" Dotty said. "There ain't nothing they can do for that man that we can't. And we can give him love!"

"Really, Dotty," said Ralph Dalton, putting a hand on his wife's shoulder. Two against one. "Let's be sensible. You have no legal claim on Jared whatsoever. The law is completely on our side."

"I answer to a higher law," Dotty said, as sure as sunset. "That man in there is family now sure as I'm standing here. The good Lord gave him to us for better or worse. Package deal."

"He'll like Kennsington," Stephen's mother went on. "The Hails and the Van Wycks both put their parents in the same home where Jared will be staying. They just loved it."

"He ain't going to love it," Dotty said, plunking a box of vanilla wafers out on the table.

Dotty was right. Grandad would hate that fancy nursing home as much as Orphan would have hated Dalton Stables. Grandad didn't belong there. He belonged with us—for better or worse.

"Well," Ralph Dalton cut in, "even if Jared doesn't *love* it, what other choice do we have?"

"To leave him here!" Dotty shouted.

"We can't do that, Dotty," he said. "Not now."

"Why not now? Why the rush to get him out of here all of a sudden?" Dotty marched over to stand inches from Ralph Dalton, who towered over her, Goliath to her David.

"I think you know why, Dotty," he said. "We can't allow Jared to keep wandering off. He could be seriously hurt next time. Or he could seriously hurt someone else. He hurt Scoop this time. What about the next time? Are you willing to let him hurt B.C. or a perfect stranger?"

"I'd like to know who it was told you our personal business!" Dotty said, as angry as I'd ever seen her.

I couldn't stand the silence. Couldn't stand the question. Couldn't stand the answer. "Me!" I yelled, rushing between Dotty and Ralph Dalton and turning my back on him. "It was me, Dotty! Me."

In the silence of the kitchen, I could hear the buzz of the refrigerator, a door lightly shutting somewhere, a dog barking in the distance. Dotty looked as if I'd punched her in the stomach.

Stephen Dalton came up behind me. "Scoop, what are you doing? You're blowing the whole thing! What's the matter with you?"

"*I* told them about Grandad," I said, ignoring everyone except Dotty and trying not to cry. "It's my fault. I wanted them to take him."

"Oh, Scoop," Dotty said, her eyes soft as honey, "why didn't you say nothing to me?"

"I don't know, Dotty. I was mad at Grandad. I know it wasn't his fault, but I blamed him for everything I missed out on. So I told Stephen in church. I didn't mean to, not really. But in a way ... I guess I did. I guess I hoped he'd tell his folks and they'd take Grandad off our hands. I'm so sorry, Dotty."

I walked over to the Daltons. Stephen's mom sat stiffly in our only good kitchen chair, and his dad had moved behind her, standing just as stiff. "But I changed my mind," I cried, searching their faces for a glimmer of understanding. "I don't want you to take Grandad away. He belongs here! I want him to stay with us and—"

"Dotty! Scoop!" B.C. shouted from the doorway, where he must have been standing for a while, trying to get our attention.

We turned toward him.

B.C. stared past everybody and straight into my eyes when he said, "Grandad's gone."

18

Grandad can't be gone," Dotty said. But she pushed past B.C. and ran toward Grandad's room.

I passed her and burst into his room first. The stench of rotten food and old age flooded over me, almost pressing me out of the room, as if there were no more air inside. I stared at his empty bed, the covers neatly turned back. His shoes and his slippers were still under the bed, and his bathrobe was gone.

Patricia Dalton gasped behind me. "Where could he be?"

"I'll check the bathroom," said her husband.

We searched the house upstairs and down, then raced outside in the cold rain. "Grandad!" I yelled at the top of my lungs. The only answer came in other shouts pleading for Grandad in the names he'd acquired over the years: "Jared!" "Daddy!" "Dad Coop!" "Grandad!"

The wind tore the leaves off the trees and threw them at us as we spread out across the lawn to look for him.

"What should we do?" Patricia whined when we'd quickly covered the area around our house.

"Let's split up and hunt," Dotty said. "No telling where he's got off to."

But I knew. I knew where he'd head as sure as if I'd seen him go. There was no telling how far he might have gotten already. But I thought I knew where to find him. And I wanted to be the one to find him. This was all my fault. I had to find my grandad and tell him I was sorry.

"I'll go to Horsefeathers and get Orphan," I told Dotty. "I'll find him, Dotty. I'm so sorry."

"You pray now, hear?" Dotty said. "And don't you go blaming yourself."

I ran so hard to Horsefeathers that my sides ached and my eyes stung from the rain. My broken arm kept slowing me down, making it hard to run fast.

The outside light lit up a narrow line into the paddock at Horsefeathers. Clouds of raindrops danced suspended in the pale yellow light. The pounding of the rain on the barn roof drowned out Orphan's greeting. I clipped a lead rope to Orphan's halter and opened the gate.

With one bum arm, I'd never be able to swing up on Orphan. I had to use a stump to mount bareback.

"Come on, Girl," I whispered to her as I slid onto her wet back, grabbing on to a lock of mane with my right hand while the rope settled between my fingers. "Let's go find Grandad."

The rain slowed to a cold mist that seeped into my bones. A fog hung over everything, making me feel as if Orphan and I were completely alone, the only living creatures on earth. I prayed and asked God to forgive me for being so selfish and to help me find my grandfather.

Orphan seemed to understand exactly where I wanted to go. She headed straight through the pasture toward Grandad's old house. I felt her stepping carefully in the mud, setting her hooves sure and solid. Her wet horse fur smelled warm and clean, and I leaned forward on her neck. Tiny drops of rain felt like pin pricks on my cheeks. My sore arm twitched with flashes of pain. I didn't care. I just wanted to get to Grandad.

Grandad's old house lay ahead of us through the mist. A shutter banged on the far side of the broken-down building, a steady slapping against the rotting wood.

Orphan stopped outside the cellar door. I managed to slide off my horse, but my foot slipped in the mud and I fell backwards, landing on my seat. I didn't hit my arm, but the jarring must have set it off and the throbbing seemed to swell from my fingertips to my shoulder.

"Stay!" I told Orphan, struggling to my feet. I let the lead rope drop to the muddy ground. Orphan sneezed and stamped the mud, splattering me.

The gray darkness turned to black as I felt my way down the cellar steps. Something light and sticky brushed my face, a spider web. My free hand slid on the slippery, cellar wall as I took another step down. It smelled like well water and rotting vegetables, the odor growing stronger with every step down. I could have been descending into a bottomless cave, a pit, a dungeon with no end.

At the bottom of the stairs I tripped on something, but felt the dirt floor under my feet. I knew there was a light bulb overhead if I could just find the string to pull it on. I swiped the black air until I felt the string swing back and forth out of my grasp.

My foot kicked something and I heard it break. It sounded like glass. I hoped Grandad hadn't come here barefoot.

"Grandad! Grandad?" I hollered.

Nobody answered, but I sensed that somebody was there.

"It's okay, Grandad," I said, feeling for the overhead light string. It grazed my fingertips as it swung by, teasing me. I reached for it, but it slipped between my fingers before I could grab it.

"You're going to be okay, Grandad. You're coming home with Dotty and B.C. and me. It's all going to be okay."

Outside a car door slammed, and shouts

blew above the ground like the wind. Orphan whinnied and someone yelled, "They're down here!"

Reaching up on my tiptoes, I waved my good arm above my head, dreading spider webs and unseen terrors. I felt the string, closed my fingers around it, and gave it a big yank. Its brightness forced my eyes shut.

The first thing I saw when I opened my eyes was a stack of glass jars on the cellar floor. Jars and jars and jars of nothing.

And then I saw him—Grandad Coop lying on the floor, curled up and surrounded by empty jars. He looked like an angel, more peaceful than I'd ever seen him. His eyes were closed, and the corners of his mouth turned up slightly in a secret grin, as if he'd just seen someone he had-n't seen in a long, long time.

Outside, Orphan nickered and the wind howled. I heard footsteps on the stairs and my own sobs as I stared down at my grandfather, lying at my feet, dead in the middle of a glass jar ocean.

19

I knelt down beside Grandad and smoothed the tufts of gray hair that stuck out on the sides of his head. "I'm sorry, Grandad," I said, the tears flowing down my cheeks onto his wrinkled face. "I'm so sorry."

I don't know how long I stayed there on my knees. Eventually I felt a hand on my shoulder and heard Dotty say something to God. She squeezed my shoulder. "He's with Jesus now, Honey. He ain't got no more pain or trouble."

But I couldn't stop crying.

I backed away from Grandad when Stephen's mother came. She squatted beside her father and leaned her head down to his. Her shoulders shook as she hugged my grandfather, while Stephen and his father looked on quietly and the wind rattled the cellar door as if somebody was trying to get in or go out.

~~~~~~~~~~~~~~~~~~~~~~~~~~~~~~~

B.C. and I stayed home from school on Monday and Tuesday. Dotty didn't cry all the time, but red lines marked the whites of her eyes like highway squiggles on a roadmap. Maggie and Jen called, and even Carla Buckingham called long distance from Lexington, Kentucky. But I didn't go to the phone.

Dotty tried to talk to me a couple of times to tell me none of it was my fault. I thought some of it probably was. But I couldn't sort out where all my bad feelings were coming from. I did feel guilty. I wondered if Grandad had known what we were all fighting about that last night. I wondered if he'd had any idea that I'd told on him to Stephen.

But more than the guilt, I felt a loss. I'd lost Grandad. Part of Grandad had been lost to me a long time ago. Part of him I'd never come close to having. And that was the worst loss—that I'd never even known much about my grandfather. And now I never would.

My brother surprised me and turned out to be a much better help to Dotty than I was in getting the funeral together. The phone seemed to ring all the time. B.C. would answer it before the second ring. Sometimes he'd just listen for a long time, then hang up. Other times he'd holler for Dotty.

~~~~~~~~~~~~~~~~~~~~~~~~~~~~~~~

The morning of the funeral, B.C. came to my room. "Scoop?" he whispered. "You asleep?"

I'd been awake almost all night. I turned toward B.C. and sat up in bed. "I'm up, B.C.," I said. "Come on in."

Through the window nothing but gray showed. It could have been 5:30 in the morning or 5:30 at night. It didn't matter.

"Do you think Grandad is in heaven?" he asked, not looking at me as he sat at the foot of my bed.

"Yeah," I said. But I remembered how hard Dotty had tried to talk to Grandad about Jesus. I wondered if we'd ever know whether she got through to him or not.

"So ..." B.C. said, running his finger around a square in my patchwork quilt, "... does that mean he's in the same place as our folks?"

I'd been thinking about them a lot too, our folks. I studied B.C., who looked about 7 years old instead of 9. Nine years old and already he'd lost a mother, a father, and the only grandparent he ever had.

"I think it does mean that, B.C.," I said. "I'll bet our dad was waiting right at the pearly gates of heaven for Grandad. And Mom too. And Reba, your grandma." I tried to imagine that reunion—Grandad smiling at them, but with a full set of gleaming white teeth. And Mom and Dad looking just like they did in the wedding picture on my dresser, only newer somehow. Then I threw in the two babies who died before my folks adopted me and had B.C. I wondered if the babies would still be babies, or if they'd be big yet.

B.C. hopped off my bed. "Okay then," he said. And he left.

~~~~~~~~~~~~~~~~~~~~~~~~~~~~~~~~

I took a long, hot bath and sank deep into the water until it wrinkled my skin. My finger itched, and my arm felt good out of the sling.

Dotty knocked on the door. "Scoop! Hurry up! We have to leave for church in 20 minutes."

I dreaded Grandad's funeral. I wondered if our pastor knew Grandad any better than I did. I tried to call up every story I'd ever heard about my grandfather. I didn't even know how he met his wife, and neither did Dotty when I asked her. What had he been thinking about when he started his horse farm? When he got married to Reba? When he had a son and named him Benjamin? When he had grandchildren? I wished I'd taken the time to ask him.

Dotty pounded on the bathroom door until I got out. "I'm coming!" I hollered back. Only then did I think about what I was going to wear. I hadn't been to a funeral since my parents died. There had been a couple of funerals Dotty had tried to get me to go to at our church, but in the end I'd won out. I didn't want to be reminded of my parents' funeral. Already it felt as if Mom and

Dad were dying again along with Grandad, that somehow they'd be sharing his funeral.

"There's a dress laid out on the bed for you, Scoop," Dotty said when I opened the door, wrapped in a beach towel. "Skedaddle on up and put it on. We have to go now!"

The dress was really a black skirt, a very long skirt, and a black blouse. I wondered where Dotty had found such an old-fashioned outfit. Or who had given it to her. Any other day I wouldn't have put it on no matter how much Dotty begged me. But I figured Dotty didn't deserve any more trouble than I'd already given her.

I got dressed, pinning the elastic waist so the skirt wouldn't fall down. Then I hustled downstairs to find B.C. sitting stiff as Grandad in the old rocking chair and staring at the blank TV screen.

Dotty drove B.C. and me to the funeral, and we picked up the Hat Lady on the way. Mrs. Powers tried to talk to us, turning around from the front seat so it looked like the flowers on her hat swayed in the breeze as she rotated. But B.C. wasn't any more talkative than I was, and she gave up before we crossed Main Street.

Ray came up to the car in the parking lot of the church and opened my back door. "Sorry, Scoop," he said. He looked as uncomfortable in his black suit as B.C.

"Thanks, Ray," I said, not looking at him,

knowing I'd burst out crying if he looked like he felt pity for me.

Ray leaned into the backseat of the car, where B.C. still sat. He hadn't moved an inch toward getting out of the car. "Hey, B.C.," Ray said, so kind it made me want to cry again. "Come on out, Buddy."

And B.C. came out. I knew there had been every chance B.C. would have stayed right there in the backseat of Dotty's car, refusing to come inside, if it hadn't been for Ray.

"Thank You, Lord," Dotty said, smiling at Ray.

We walked across the parking lot. Mrs. Powers' high heels clicked and echoed through the mist. The fog had grown so thick that I couldn't see through to the end of the parking lot. But I could see enough to know there'd be plenty of empty seats at the funeral. Only six or seven cars were parked close to the church. I wasn't the only one who had never gotten to know Grandad.

Maggie 37 Black and Jen Zucker came down the aisle and hugged me, one on each side, making it a sandwich hug. They hugged Dotty and B.C. Maggie was crying, and her tears looked real.

"Sorry, Scoop," Jen said. "When you feel like it, I'll help you make up the school you missed."

I tried to smile thanks.

"Thank you for coming, girls," Dotty said, reaching into her purse for another handkerchief. "That was real nice of you." She pulled out a big, white handkerchief that used to be Grandad's. She stared at it a minute, then stuffed it back in her bag without using it.

I was glad Dotty thanked my friends for coming because I just couldn't. I was hanging on by a thread, trying not to break down and cry. I felt like one of Grandad's jars, only so full of ice-cold water that if one more drop got through, I'd spill out of myself—start crying and never stop.

Mr. and Mrs. Zucker came over to us, and Mr. Zucker offered his "condolences," whatever they were. Tommy Zucker kept staring at me. The twins hit each other and one of the triplets was crying. Travis lightly punched me in the shoulder and didn't say anything. I swallowed to keep the tears down. Ray stood on my other side and touched my finger with the stitches in it. Then they all drifted to seats somewhere.

Mrs. Hathaway, who's about 200 years old, played the organ, a choppy, slow dirge that would have made you know you were at a funeral even if you couldn't see anything else. I wished she would play something faster, like the William Tell Overture—"The Lone Ranger's Song," Grandad called it whenever he heard it at a horse show.

B.C. was tugging at me. Maggie and Jen slid into the pew behind the first row, where B.C., Dotty, and me and the Daltons had to sit. Stephen and his parents occupied front row center, which was fine with me. Dotty was inching up toward the open casket.

"Are you going closer?" B.C. asked, still pulling on my blouse. "I want to see Grandad closeup."

I shook off his grip. "I'm not going up there, B.C.," I said. "Go ahead if you want to. Go with Dotty."

I could see Grandad well enough from where I was standing. Too well. He was dressed in a black suit. I'd never seen him wearing a suit when he was alive. I wondered where Dotty got it, or if the funeral director just had them on hand.

Even from where I stood several yards away, I could tell that the smile on his face took somebody a lot of work, more work than Grandad had given his smile in the years I'd been around. He looked like he was made of wax. It wasn't Grandad up there. I didn't have to see his shell to know he wasn't there anymore. I squeezed my eyes shut and prayed that Grandad was up in heaven, smiling a real smile at my mom and dad and grandma, shaking their heads at us way down here and laughing about how little we understood about things like life ... and death.

20

"S coop, come sit down over this way, Hon," Dotty said, putting one arm around my good shoulder and guiding me to the pew. It felt wrong. Our normal pew was back farther and to the left. B.C. scooched over so Dotty could sit between us. I was used to Grandad sitting on my left in church, walled in so he wouldn't get up and wander.

"Don't your grandad look nice?" Dotty asked, folding her hands and unfolding them again in her lap. I hadn't noticed before, but she was wearing a navy dress I'd never seen. She kept tugging at the hem that fell to her mid calf. "He looks like an angel."

People came over to our pew. Maggie's step-dad, Mr. Chesley, leaned into our pew and reached across me to shake or take Dotty's hand. "I'm sorry for your loss," he whispered.

Other people came over and said how sorry they were. They patted B.C. on the head and told him his grandad had gone to a better place. They told Dotty that if she needed anything,

anything at all, she should call. Me, they left alone. I must have had a glass window face that let everybody see into me and realize I didn't want to talk to anybody.

We stood when the music started for "Amazing Grace." I heard the familiar tune, but nothing felt real to me. Before I started singing, the hymn was over and I felt Dotty at my arm, pulling me to sit down again.

"People," said our pastor, Pastor Dan, clearing his throat over the microphone, which he probably wouldn't have needed for this small group. "Brothers and Sisters in Christ." He wore a black robe that didn't show how thin he was. Dotty always wanted to take him home with us and fatten him up. Brown shoes with dark brown tassels stuck out beneath his robe. B.C. and I used to crack each other up guessing what he really wore under that robe.

I'd always imagined that Pastor Dan was the exact same age my dad would be if he were still alive. They were probably pretty close in age anyway. When Pastor Dan started losing his hair, I imagined my dad going bald. But they didn't look anything alike. Benjamin Coop wasn't a farmer, but he looked like one. I still remember the rough, scratchy feel of his palm when he held my hand. Pastor Dan's hands gleamed soft and almost white as he held out his hands to welcome the mourners.

He stepped down from the pulpit to stand in front of the congregation, right between Daltons and us. "We are gathered together here to honor the man known to many of you as Jared Coop." He looked back and forth from us to the Daltons, as if he couldn't decide who he was talking to. "What do we know about this man who walked our town for over 80 years? He was a son himself once, a husband, a father, a grandfather—and from what I hear, a pretty fair horse trader in his day."

A sprinkling of low laughter seasoned the sanctuary.

"Jared Coop," Pastor Dan continued, "was all these things ... and much, much more. So much more that none of us may ever realize everything that made him who he was. He survived the Great Depression of America. He fought for our country in one world war and witnessed too many other wars as well. He experienced all the joy of love, marriage, and births. And he experienced the tragedies of life as well—failure, loss, and death, death of his beloved wife, death of his only son."

My throat felt so tight it hurt. I could hardly breathe. As often as I'd thought about my dad's death and how much B.C. and I lost in that bottle plant explosion that took both of our parents, I don't think I'd ever thought about Grandad's loss. He lost his only son.

The pastor talked on, and my mind floated in and out of the flow of his words. He mentioned all the pieces that made up my grandfather's puzzle. "Jared Coop lived a full life. Not everything that happened to him was good or happy or wanted. But everything worked together to make up the whole of his earthly gift from God—the gift of Jared Coop's life. As Romans 3:28 says, 'In all things God works for the good of those who love Him.' And verse 37 says, 'In all these things we are more than conquerors through Him who loved us.' God loves us so much He conquered death to give us the promise of eternal life with Him after the whole of this earthly life—good and bad—is finished."

Pastor Dan never said the words *package deal*, but the words were there, invisible, floating in the church air. He was saying what Dotty always said, that life is a package deal with good and bad. But this time I understood what Dotty meant all the time—that God's working even through the bad.

I heard a low jingling, and for a minute I wondered if I were imagining the sound. Then I recognized the familiar clinking of B.C.'s pocketful of bottle caps bumping against each other. When I turned to shush him, he wasn't there. For a fraction of a second, in a wave of panic, I thought he was gone—gone for good, just like Grandad.

Then I saw my brother walk right past the pastor to get to Grandad's coffin. Pastor Dan had just said "Amen" and looked up to see B.C. tiptoeing past him up the steps to the plain, brown coffin.

Nobody made a sound as little B.C. smiled down at Grandad. Pastor Dan turned his back to us and became a spectator just like the rest of us.

B.C. reached into his pocket and pulled out his bottle caps. "These are for you, Grandad," B.C. said, as if Grandad were alive and they were the only two people on earth who were. "You can play with them. Share them with my folks in heaven. Tell my dad I still love every bottle cap he ever gave me."

I couldn't keep it in any longer. Tears pushed their way out of me with such force that my whole body shook. I couldn't sit there and do this. I shouldn't have come to the funeral. Grandad wouldn't even have wanted me at his funeral. I didn't belong.

I burst out of the pew. With my good hand over my mouth, I ran up the aisle. Several people called my name, but I kept running—out of church, down the steps, across the lawn, and into the fog.

21

Without a conscious decision, I was running down the road away from church and toward Horsefeathers. My feet moved without me, not stopping until I saw the barn and the fences, the paddock and my horse.

Orphan whinnied and tossed her head, running over to meet me at the paddock fence. I climbed the fence and sat on the top rail. Orphan put her head in my lap. I buried my face in her warm fur and cried. We stayed that way, her head in my lap, my head resting against her, until she was wet with my tears.

"Orphan, Orphan," I whispered. "I never even knew him—not really. Not the whole package. And now I never will."

I wanted to have pictures in my memory of the way Grandad had looked before I met him. I wanted to picture him the way he'd been when my parents first adopted me and brought me to his horse farm so they could "show me off." He'd been trying to give his new mixed-breed foal a bottle, since her mother had just died foaling. That filly was Orphan. Grandad was the one who let me try to get the feeble black foal to take the bottle. And that's when Orphan and I became partners.

But when I let my mind try to think about Grandad, instead of picturing the younger, stronger grandfather, all I could see was Grandad the way he had been at the end, when the Alzheimer's disease made him do crazy things. I pictured him in our kitchen dumping out pickles onto the floor for me to clean up, hoarding his dirty jars, fighting me for empty glass containers.

Horsefeathers! Those blasted jars. Why did he want them? What was it about those glass containers? Why did he run off to the cellar every time he got the chance? Why had he died surrounded by a sea of glass jars? Stupid glass jars.

I had to know. I had to understand.

I stood on the rail fence and slid onto Orphan's back, scooting my long black skirt under me. I didn't even put the lead rope on Orphan's halter but urged her around the paddock at a canter. We gained speed until I squeezed in with my knees. "Jump, Orphan!" I commanded.

Orphan sailed over the paddock fence and landed with a smooth thump in the south pasture. She headed straight for Grandad's old house without any signal from me. We raced as if we were searching urgently for Grandad again. But this time I knew we wouldn't find him.

Still, I had to go. There had to be a clue in his old cellar. Why else would he have fought so hard to get back there? I hugged Orphan's broad neck and let her wet, black mane swish in my face as we cantered through the gray fog, the mist pricking us like wet dust particles.

I didn't see the house until we were right up on it. The mist and fog mingled so closely the house seemed to have steam pouring from it.

"Whoa, Orphan," I said. I'd almost forgotten my arm was still in a sling until I started to dismount. I had to swing my right leg over her neck to the opposite side so I was sitting sideways on my horse. Then I jumped down to the ground. The jarring when I landed shook my arm and made it throb with pain. "Stay here, Girl," I whispered to Orphan.

Mist covered me like a soft, down blanket as I walked toward the cellar. The door was cocked open just as it had been when I'd found Grandad at the bottom of the stairs. My heart pounded as I set one foot on the top step. I half-expected to see him there again—or still. The light was on, amazingly still shining from the overhead bulb.

I eased down one step, then another, steadying myself with one hand along the cold, clammy cement wall. It still smelled putrid and dank.

There it was, just like I'd left it—a virtual nest

of glass jars. Only the nest was empty. If I closed my eyes I could see Grandad curled up in the center of all those jars, smiling like an angel.

I stepped closer, glancing from jar to jar, years worth of Mason jars my grandmother probably used to do canning. There were old pickle jars too, a tiny mustard container, weird-shaped bottles, a lifetime collection of glass containers.

Why?

I dropped down to my knees and touched the nearest jar, the glass cool to my fingers. Next to me on the cold, damp cement floor was broken glass. I remembered kicking something over when I'd reached for the light bulb the night I found Grandad. It looked like two jars had crashed and broken.

I picked up a piece of glass and noticed a small piece of paper the size of an address label. It was lying in the middle of broken glass.

I reached for the paper and pulled it out of the debris. It was folded over once and had yellowed and cracked. Dried tape stuck to it. I unfolded the strip of paper and saw there was something typed on it. Flattening the paper out, I held it to the light and read:

Air from a perfect sunrise as Reba smiled at me in a glance over her shoulder—May 3, 1958.

I read the note again. Reba. Grandad's wife. I shivered from the warmth, not the cold, passing through me, as if I too were feeling that sunrise and seeing the smile on the face of the grandmother I'd never met.

I'd broken two jars that night. Maybe ... I fingered through the broken glass and found another silver metal lid to a broken jar. Slowly I turned over the lid. A folded piece of paper was stuck to the inside of this lid too. I touched the old piece of paper, and it fell off, the glue long ago dried up like my grandfather's wrinkled skin.

My heart pounded as I unfolded the slip of paper and read it:

The smell of rain in Ada, North Dakota, May 19, 1942.

I breathed in the air around the broken glass. I could almost smell that Dakota rain. I'd never known that Grandad made it all the way to North Dakota.

I grabbed another jar and turned it over. There it was—another piece of paper stuck to the inside of the lid. I checked another jar and another. Each one had a secret label.

Air! Grandad had cried. *I need air!*

Of course. He needed *this* air. *His* air. My grandfather had collected air. He wasn't crazy! He knew exactly what he was doing when he escaped to this cellar. Here in these time-worn jars was the air of a lifetime.

22

S coop! Are you down there?" The voice sounded so far away, miles away, years away. "Scoop?" A car door slammed, then another.

I heard footsteps on the stairs and looked up to see Travis Zucker, with Ray behind him. They looked at me as if what they saw scared them.

"Are you okay, Scoop?" Travis asked, coming down a step at a time. "Your Aunt Dotty sent us to find you. She ... well, we were all pretty worried when you took off like that."

I was crying and laughing at the same time and couldn't get words out.

Ray and Travis exchanged worried glances.

"Is she down there?" Jen Zucker in a yellow rain slicker appeared in the cellar doorway, casting her shadow on the stairs. She pushed past Travis and Ray and made her way through the jars to me. "Scoop?"

"Be careful!" I shouted.

Jen stopped as if I'd hit her. Her eyes grew big and her hand went to her throat.

"The jars, Jen," I said calmly. "Don't knock

over the jars. That's all I meant. I'm okay. Really. These are Grandad's jars."

They didn't answer. I could imagine what they thought seeing me in Grandad's glass jar nest. But I didn't have time to straighten them out. Not just yet. "I need your help," I said. Jen knelt down beside me and smoothed my hair out of my face. "That's why we came, Scoop," she said in the voice she uses to coax the twins to go to bed. "Dotty wants us to bring you back. We can still meet everybody at the cemetery."

Travis spoke up. "I think Dotty would understand if you're not up to going to the gravesite though. Would you like me to give you a lift home, Scoop? Jen could stay with you until Dotty gets back."

Jen nodded. "Good idea, Travis."

"No! I want to go to the cemetery," I said. My heart and mind were racing. "I need all of you to help me with these jars." I stood up and took four of the Mason jars in my arms, balancing them on my sling. Carefully I weaved through Ray and Travis on the stairs. The boys stared silently at me as I passed them.

"Don't just stand there!" I ordered. "We need to load all of these jars into the truck. Go! Trust me. Please! I know what I'm doing. And be careful!"

I turned and locked stares with Ray. His big

cow eyes stared back. Finally, he said. "Where do you want them?"

Travis laid down an old blanket in the back of the truck. We loaded all of the jars on top of that, dozens and dozens of glass jars in all sizes and shapes.

"Careful!" I cautioned, hugging my own load of jars close to me, the way Grandad had done those last days. He was right. These jars were precious.

The fog rolled in deeper than before. By the time we finished loading every last jar into Travis's pickup, it was hard to see the house.

"Ray," I said, as he closed the truck bed. "You ride back here with these jars and hold onto them. Travis, you better drive slow and easy. I don't want even one jar broken."

"What about you, Scoop?" Jen asked, her face wrinkled in worry so that she looked like the littlest Zucker baby when he was born after 23 hours of labor.

"Orphan and I will meet you at the cemetery," I said.

They argued with me. They wanted me to ride with them. Ray said he'd lead Orphan back to Horsefeathers. But it was no use. I had my mind made up. I had never felt more connected with my grandfather or more in tune with God. Prayers of thankfulness were swimming through my mind, making their way to God. I knew I was doing what God and Grandad wanted me to do.

Travis gave me a boost up on Orphan, who had waited patiently for me through the whole ordeal. Jen found a piece of twine in the truck and tied it onto Orphan's halter for reins. She handed the twine up to me. "Be careful, Scoop," she said.

I thanked them and took off into the fog. I just hoped I wouldn't be too late.

~~~~~~~~~~~~~~~~~~~~~~~~~~~~~~

Orphan and I made good time through the pastures by cutting across neighboring farms. Taking a shortcut past the old train tracks, we came out on the far side of the cemetery.

When I spotted a pocket of black umbrellas in the middle of the cemetery, I slid off Orphan and walked up to them, sloshing through the muddy grass. Orphan followed so close behind me I could feel her breath on my neck.

Dotty came running toward me, letting her umbrella fall to the ground. B.C. trailed right behind her. "Scoop!" Dotty yelled, waving at me like she thought I might run away again. She threw her arms around me. "Thank You, Jesus, for keeping her safe!" Dotty declared, sounding out of breath. "I didn't know where you was, Scoop. When you tore out of the church like that, you scared the living daylights out of me!"

I hugged her back. "I'm sorry, Dotty," I said. And I was. I didn't want to give Dotty any more grief than she already had. I looked down at B.C., who was totally quiet, staring at me like I had two heads. "I'm okay, B.C.," I said. "Don't look so worried. I was with Orphan. She took good care of me."

"I gave Grandad my best bottle caps," my brother said softly.

"I saw, B.C.," I said. "That was real nice of you." I smiled at him, and he returned my grin.

Travis' white pickup appeared out of the mist, winding toward us on the road from the front cemetery gate.

"Dotty," I said, moving toward the cluster of umbrellas gathered around the open grave. Grandad's closed casket rested on a green carpet that covered the rectangle hole in the ground. "I discovered something awesome, something Grandad did his whole life."

We inched back to the umbrella group. "That's fine, Scoop," Dotty said. "Do you reckon it'll hold till we're done burying your grandaddy?"

"Please, Dotty," I begged. "Wait. You have to see this. I know it's what Grandad would have wanted."

Travis backed the pickup truck close to Grandad's coffin. The stone at one end of the grave was half blank. The other side had the name of my grandmother and the dates of her birth and death before I was born.

Just to the left was the tiny grave shared by my parents. A small gray stone marked the spot and gave the bare facts: *Benjamin Coop and His Beloved Wife, Emma Eberhart Coop.*

Instead of making me want to cry like the sight of their grave usually did, it completed this moment in time. They should be here. It was right. Benjamin and Emma Coop, next to Reba Mae Eichelberger Coop, next to Jared Coop's waiting grave. It was as if their memories were all here waiting for this moment, all part of the package. I could almost feel the crowd in heaven watching us.

"Careful!" Ray shouted at Travis from his perch in the back of the muddy white pickup truck. Poor Ray was soaking wet, hunched over armloads of jars, his long legs spread-eagled to hold more jars steady as Travis bumped backwards. Jen stuck her head out the window and told Travis when to stop.

Travis and Jen got out of the truck and walked back to Ray and the jars. The few people who had followed Dotty to the cemetery now huddled close around the back of the pickup. Maggie 37 and her stepfather walked up to Dotty and me.

"Scoop?" Maggie asked, her eyes wide with questions she didn't ask.

"It's okay, Maggie. You'll see. Look at what Grandad did!" We all circled the pickup and stared in at the glass jars sitting in the truck bed.

"What is this stuff, Scoop?" It was Stephen Dalton, standing between his parents. His mother held a hankie to her eyes.

"What's going on?" Ralph Dalton asked sharply before I could answer Stephen.

"Mr. and Mrs. Dalton, Stephen, I know this looks weird, but I think this is what Grandad would have wanted." I looked directly at each one of them, praying God would show me how to do what I wanted to do next. And praying that God would make them understand, would help us all understand.

23

W hat do want us to do, Scoop?" Travis
asked.

"Will you unload the jars and spread them
around Grandad's grave, please?" I asked.

Ray and Travis began unloading the jars two
at a time. Then Jen and Maggie joined in.

"Scoop, Honey," Dotty said, feeling my
forehead with her rough, thick hand, "are you
sure you know what you're doing?"

"I do, Dotty. I finally do."

I hate speaking in a crowd, much less speaking *to* a crowd, but the words were pushing up
from somewhere inside me. They had to get out.
I looked around the circle of astonished faces—
the Daltons, Pastor Dan, the Hat Lady, Mr. Ford
and Lou from Hy-Klas.

"Horsefeathers," I said. "I'm sorry about all
this." I cleared my throat to make me louder.
Orphan nickered from somewhere behind me.
Rain gently splattered stones, sounding like
somebody typing in a room far away.

"Remember what Pastor Dan said about Grandad's whole life, the whole package?" I said. "That's what I wanted to know about. That's what I thought was lost forever—the pieces of the puzzle that made up my grandfather. But it's not lost! Grandad saved it."

Ray and Travis set down the last of the jars, which formed a glass frame around the rectangular hole in the ground.

I swallowed and prayed God would give me the right words. "Lately, because of his Alzheimer's disease, my grandad wasn't himself. We all thought he was just a little crazy when he'd run off and end up at his old house. He didn't go inside the house though. He'd run straight to the cellar, straight to these jars. But Grandad wasn't crazy."

Dotty smiled and nodded an *Amen* at me. B.C. was holding her hand. I don't think either one of them had ever thought Grandad was crazy.

I walked over to the jars and knelt down by the closest ones. People shifted so they could see. B.C. came and knelt beside me. Then Dotty did too.

"In each of these jars," I said, "is air!" I held one jar up above my head and saw all eyes focus on it. "Air Grandad collected over years and years of living. He captured air and kept it in jars labeled to remind him of moments in his life.

These jars are like a living scrapbook of his whole life—the whole package."

Nobody spoke. The cemetery was as quiet as the mist. "When I found Grandad at the bottom of the cellar steps, I accidentally knocked over a couple of jars. This afternoon when I ran out of church, I ended up in Grandad's cellar searching for whatever he had searched for there. And while I was down there among his jars—jars I'd figured were empty—I found this."

I brought out the yellowed paper. "This was in the glass. But it had been folded up a long, long time ago and taped to the inside of the jar, on the underside of the metal lid."

I unrolled the wad of paper, glanced at Dotty and B.C., and read: "It says, *Air from a perfect sunrise as Reba smiled at me in a glance over her shoulder—May 3, 1958.*"

I heard Dotty gasp beside me. "Oh, Jared," she said.

"This was in another jar," I said, unfolding the second slip of paper:

"The smell of rain in Ada, North Dakota, May 19, 1942."

"Don't you see?" I pleaded. "Grandad Coop saved air like memory. He stored his moments in glass jars."

Patricia Dalton moved in and knelt beside us. She touched one of the jars with her gloved finger. "I remember these old jars," she said, half smiling, half crying. "We always thought they were antique glass or something the way he guarded them. He never let us kids touch them or even go near them."

"Listen," I said to her after a minute. "Grandad was your father so you should be the one to do the deciding. But I think Grandad would want us to free the air in these jars, to let his memories out free, like he is now. Still, I won't do it unless you say so."

She glanced over her shoulder at her husband, then at Stephen. Then she looked back at me. "Go ahead, Scoop. Please."

The first jar I opened was gray with age. B.C. had to help me get the lid off, holding the jar with two hands so I could twist the lid with one. I made my brother cover the mouth of the jar with his hand until I could read the label.

Everyone leaned in and strained to hear what Grandad had to say. I unfolded the paper and read: *"Stale air of Dec. 7, 1941, the day Pearl Harbor was bombed."*

B.C. slid his hand off the rim of the jar, letting the stale air rise free above us. In silence, we breathed the same air Americans had breathed on the day a foreign nation bombed our country. I imagined exploding bombs booming, the screams of alarm, the wailing of grief-stricken families.

Dotty opened the next jar and passed me the

paper on the inside lid. I read it aloud: *"Burning leaves Oct. 28, 1949, watching Reba jump into a freshly raked pile."*

Patricia Dalton laughed, then sobbed quietly. I offered her the next jar, but she smiled and pushed it back to me.

"First spring rain on a brand-new foal, 1939."

I glanced at Orphan, who watched us patiently. I could smell her wet fur—unless it was the first spring rain on a new foal in 1939 I was smelling.

Jar after jar, memories spilled out over the cemetery. There was air from the wedding day of Reba and Jared Coop. Air from the hopeful day they bought their farm in West Salem. Air from the evening they sold their watches and wedding rings to buy their first horse.

Halfway through the jars, I opened a slip of paper and asked B.C. to move over by Patricia Dalton before taking his hand away. "This one says: *Air on the morning God gave me a beautiful daughter, Patricia."*

B.C. moved his hand away when the mouth of the jar was inches from Patricia Dalton's mouth. Stephen's mother closed her eyes and breathed in the air as if she could feel the breeze. She sobbed in gentle, soft sounds that sounded mixed with as much pleasure as pain. She took the jar from B.C. and hugged it against her.

I opened the next jar, and it said: *"Air on the day I became a grandfather to Stephen Dalton."* B.C. handed the jar to Stephen, and I think Stephen was crying.

I could almost hear the laughter as we freed the air in a jar labeled: *My son Benjamin's laughter on his 15th birthday.* My age. I could feel Grandad's sorrow when he captured the air on the day my dad was killed. The pain of it felt familiar as bone, always there just under the surface.

Dotty opened the next jar and handed me the paper. All it said was: *Minnie Johnson likes me back.* The date on the paper made it the oldest jar yet.

"Who was Minnie Johnson?" I asked.

Dotty shrugged and shook her head.

I turned to Patricia Dalton, but she shook her head too. "I have no idea," she said.

"Jared would have been a boy then," said Ralph Dalton.

Something about the fact that nobody knew who this woman— this girl—had been, made me feel good inside. Minnie Johnson had meant enough to Grandad one day for him to collect her air into his life as a memory. She was a piece in his puzzle. Maybe she had been to my grandad what Jake had been to me. Maybe Minnie Johnson thought Jared Coop was *pretty cute.*

B.C. had to ask Ray to help open a small jelly jar. Ray handed the paper to me and kept his hand over the top of the jar until I read. I started to read, then stopped, as tears burned in my throat. "It says ... *A promising day for my son Benjamin in the adoption of his daughter.*" I knew that when my folks adopted me, Grandad was barely speaking to them. But he had loved them enough, loved me enough, to capture the air of that day in a glass jar.

The biggest jar still sat in front of me. I had kept reaching around it. For some reason I knew it had to be especially important. Now I steadied the big glass jar between my knees and took off the lid. Dotty slipped her chubby hand over the top, trapping the air inside until I read the label taped to the inside of the lid.

"Horsefeathers, Dotty!" I whispered. "It says: *Blessed air from the Sunday when I heard Reba sing 'The Messiah' and I trusted Jesus Christ as my Savior.*"

Dotty broke down in tears of joy. She took her hand away from the jar and held it to her face. "I knew it, Lord," she whispered, breathing in the salvation air. "I knew he was Yours."

There were jars of national triumphs and tragedies—the end of World War II and Hitler, the first manned space flight, the landing on the moon, the explosion of the Space Shuttle Challenger. There was air from the Oklahoma bombing. Air from the assassinations of President Kennedy and his brother, and Martin Luther King.

There were personal triumphs and tragedies too—births and deaths, marriages and failures, moments of intense joy and moments of unbearable pain—the whole package deal of my grandad's life on earth.

When we finished, when every jar lay open around the grave, the air swirled around us filled with laughter, smiles, death, tears, births, songs. Sunrises and sunsets blended together.

We prayed and then stood silently looking up to heaven as the gray sky crept closer to the earth and the earth's mist rose to meet it, matching gray for gray until you couldn't tell where earth left off and heaven began.

Epilogue

Dotty followed Orphan and me in the car from the cemetery to Horsefeathers. Then she and B.C. drove me home. We changed into dry clothes and then set about the job of cleaning Grandad's room. It smelled so strongly of my grandfather, it was hard to believe he would never live there again. But now we knew he was in a much better room, a mansion in heaven.

"What's this?" B.C. asked, pulling an empty jar from under Grandad's pillow.

I walked over to look at it. "Horsefeathers, B.C.!" I muttered.

The jar was the one Grandad had fought to keep the day Orphan and I found him at the cellar, the day we went on our ride. I could picture Grandad on the back of Orphan, that jar in one hand, the lid in the other, his arms held high above his head as he brought lid and jar together. He was catching the air of our ride.

I pressed the cool glass against my cheeks as tears flowed down. Inside this jar was the fresh pasture air, filled with the faint scent of smoke and Orphan's sweat, the sweet smell of clover and alfalfa.

I walked up to my room, clutching the jar as Grandad would have. I peered through that jar, full of Grandad's breath and mine, his laughter mingled with Orphan's whinny and sound of a distant crow. Carefully I set it down on my dresser. I tore off a small strip of paper from my notebook and wrote the date and the words: *Air on a perfect ride with Grandad and Orphan and God.*

When I finished writing, I taped the strip of paper to the top of Grandad's jar. Then I raced down to the kitchen and dumped out the cherry jar, rinsed it, and biked as fast as I could back to the cemetery. Holding the jar above my head just like Grandad had done on our ride, I captured the air of my Grandad's life. Determining to follow in my grandfather's footsteps, I went home and made sure I had empty jars on hand. From now on I'd be capturing the whole package of the life God would give me.

I took the jar with the air of my perfect ride with Grandad and the jar of cemetery air and placed them in the center of my dresser next to my horsefeather.

Glossary of Breeds

Following is a limited list of breeds mentioned in *Horsefeathers* books.

American Saddlebred—A refined breed ranging between 15–17 hands high, spirited and with a showy presence, carrying the head and tail high and stepping high. Three-Gaited and Five-Gaited horses are American Saddlebred.

Andalusian—Elegant Spanish horse, athletic and proud. Andalusians enjoy being the center of attention and make fine dressage horses. They are frequently used as parade and bullfighting horses.

Appaloosa—Spotted horses, colored in one of five mottled patterns: blanket, leopard, marble, snowflake, and frost. They are stock horses, with good endurance and great temperaments.

Arabian—Beautiful horses with grace and stamina; can be fiery or high-spirited.

Barb—Traditional mount of the Bedouin tribes of North Africa. They can be quick-tempered.

Belgian Workhorse—One of the world's strongest breeds, these heavy draft horses have been used for farming for centuries. They have short, compact bodies with strong legs, and they work with a willing spirit.

Brumby—Wild horses of the Australian bush, still too wild to tame.

Camargue—Known as "The White Horse of the Sea," these horses still run wild in the marshlands of France.

Clydesdale—Strong workhorses averaging 17–18 hands, characterized by a gentle look with big eyes and ears.

Cob—A short, strong, muscular horse, the Welsh Cob gives a calm, comfortable ride. The horse is so reliable, it can be used to give rides to the elderly or to people with special needs.

Connemara—A child's pony, native of Ireland. Connemaras are dependable, all-purpose horses.

The Criollo—Perhaps the hardiest breed. These horses have tremendous endurance, but an unattractive appearance.

Dartmoor Pony—Sensible ponies averaging only 12½ hands. They are very sure-footed.

Exmoor—An Old British mountain pony breed, recognized by their heavy-lidded eyes, called "toad" eyes. They are strong enough to endure long winters of cold and snow.

Falabella—The world's smallest horse, though not a pony. It measures about seven hands (28 inches) when full grown. Falabellas make great pets, although they can't be ridden.

Hackney—A show horse or pony, with high-stepping action. Hackneys make popular driving and show horses.

Lipizzaner—Powerful, famous white horses of the Spanish Riding School of Vienna, Austria. They are intelligent, willing, and born performers.

Lusitano—Strong, agile horses preferred as mounts by Portuguese bullfighters.

Morgan—The Morgan horse was the first American breed. With strength and a simple elegance and good nature, Morgan horses make ideal family horses. They can also be used for any kind of pleasure riding.

Paint—Horses with predominantly two-colored coats, spotted or splashed. A Paint Horse must meet color requirements of Pintos, but must also be purebred Quarter Horse or registered Thoroughbred. They are generally stocky and compact.

Two coloring patterns of the Paint are **ovaro**—solid coat with large splashes of white; and **tobiano**—white base coat with large patches of solid darker color.

Palomino—Horses of any breed with beautiful golden coats. The color shows up in Morgan, Quarter Horse, Saddlebred, Walking Horses, and others.

Paso Fino or **Peruvian Paso**—A tough breed with great endurance for mountain work. The Paso's natural, lateral gait is unique and gives a comfortable ride.

Percheron—Giant French draft horse. Percherons are loyal hard workers.

Pinto—A registered color breed meeting certain color qualifications, as with Paints, but not requiring a specific breeding history.

Quarter Horse—An intelligent, versatile, Western-riding or ranch horse, the fastest horse in the world for the quarter-mile. The Quarter Horse is reliable, docile, and good-natured.

Shetland Pony—At 10 hands (40 inches) or under, this pony is considered the most powerful horse in the world—for its size. Independent, headstrong, and ornery, Shetlands are not the best mounts for children.

Standardbred—Powerfully built horse used in harness racing. Standardbred horses trot or pace.

Tennessee Walking Horse—Easygoing horse with three smooth gaits, including the running walk and a rocking-chair canter. Walking Horses are believed to inherit their good nature.

Thoroughbred—Fast, sleek racing horse considered the most valuable horse in the world. They tend to be high-strung and spirited.